STR

RESEMBLANCE

THE NOVEL

AUTHOR: ALMALIK TAYLOR

Printed in the United States of America

SUMMARY

Peter Phontane, self made millionaire, founds a youth organization called "New Beginnings" through which he helps troubled teens...specifically gang bangers. Though he is completely committed to his cause Peter desires a wife. Unfortunately, he finds it very difficult to meet the multi-versatile woman he desires until he meets a married bisexual couple.

Jasmine and Tyranny, two very successful women, had been partners for approximately 5 years when they both desired to have children. However, they did not want to merely have children from a man, they wanted to add a husband to the marriage.

Ultimately, the three meet and later marry. Both women conceive shortly after, and have their babies hours apart. Two daughters were born, one to each mother, yet they're identical twins!

This Novel is dedicated:

To God, my father, who has allowed me to go through the many episodes in my life...good and bad...which shaped me into being the man he intended for me to be.

To my son, who has been the blessing who changed my life for the better forever.

Black men,

Regardless of the lack of love, respect, or credit...continue to be the MEN our community needs. Society has painted a false picture of who we are, and unfortunately there are those isolated few who continue to strengthen the propaganda. However, "the race is not given to the swift but to those who endure to the end." We must each continue to contribute to change by offering ourselves as examples, as leaders, as inspiration. Someone is always watching and being influenced by what we do, so let us be responsible in our actions...always considering that the future is molded by what's done today.

PART I

Chapter
1

Soft jazz plays inside one of the most exquisite of soul food restaurants in the city o f Los Angeles - Isabella's. Two women, Jasmine and Tyranny, sit at a corner table talking, sipping Chablis, and giggling over the many seductive stares they were receiving from men all over the restaurant. Both women are exceptionally beautiful. And though both were casually dressed, each possessed an aura of confidence and style that would draw even the attention of a blind man. The women frequently visited the restaurant, and waved in response to the winks and other gestures made toward them, yet they rarely spoke to anyone other than waiters, waitresses, or the owner, Ms. Isabella - who was an older, very pleasant West Indian woman. She often mentioned how the two ladies were not only amongst her most prestigious regulars but also her favorites.

Jasmine Ambrose is a 34 year old millionaire investment broker originally from Milwaukee but now works in Los Angeles for the multibillion-dollar investment corporation, Investicom Inc. She was being considered for a promotion to Senior Vice President of her department, but her life style which has absolutely nothing to do with her job, had aroused questions within the minds of her corporate supervisors. Though Jasmine is a black woman, and no one ever specified why her promotion was being delayed, there was no doubt in her mind of what the problem was. It had nothing to do with race. Her performance over the past years with the corporation had been eminent. She had become an estimable asset, so a detail as petty as race would not have been used as an excuse to deny her promotion. Not to mention the President of the company in addition to three of the corporation's top executives were black men. Race was infallibly not a factor. It was definitely her relationship with Tyranny that was the problem.

During the previous 5 years, Jasmine had been treated differently by her co-workers. The stares, the whispers, and the occasional dildo in the desk drawer were acts of close mindedness she had gotten used to. But now her climb up the proverbial corporate ladder was being affected. It hurt her deeply yet she would never reveal it. She was bold and strong, never allowing herself to show any type of vulnerability except when she was alone with her spouse; her best friend; her soul mate. The most gratifying aspect of her life was her marriage, and she refused to give it up for any job. It was a direct reflection of who she was and a blatant indication of the fact that she was no longer willing to hide it.

For her entire life she pretended, attempting to suppress her true feelings by dating guys she could barely stand being around.
There was the all-star point guard on her high school's basketball team, who broke up with her because she would not sleep with him. Then there was the quarterback of the football team, when she was in college, who cheated on her several times. Even her boss during her very first internship on Wall Street who was just ...ugh!

Jasmine was beautiful, and having the most popular or good looking guy was expected of her. The long wavy black hair, Coppertone complexion, Indian like facial features, light brown eyes, and perfect "beach body" dictated that she be someone she wasn't. Always being praised and acknowledged for her physical beauty was redundantly tiresome...until she met Tyranny, who loved her mind and her unnoticed gentleness, kindness, and compassion.

Tyranny Elliot is a 33 year old founder of four "Pre Madonna" hair styling and beauty salons. Though she was not quite a millionaire, her businesses combined grossed nearly $300 thousand per year...which was not bad considering she had only been in business for a little over 4years. Every year after she opened her first salon, she added another. She was remarkably business minded, in light of the fact that she put herself through a school of business while working as an exotic dancer. Not only did she acquire a BA in business but she also graduated at the top of her class. She was just as gorgeous as she was intelligent.

Her hair was close to shoulder length, brown, with a slight gold tint...hypnotizing slanted brown eyes, and an unusually smooth fudge complexion. On a scale of 1-10 she was a 12, and was often referred to as a chocolate covered hour glass.

Unlike Jasmine, ever since her teenage years, Tyranny was comfortable with her sexuality. She was attracted to women and was not afraid to let it be known. There had been a few men with whom she dated in the past she never found anything fulfilling. Tyranny was overjoyed to have met Jasmine. She loved her very much and could not even imagine living life without her. By Tyranny's own admission, Jasmine brought out the best in her.

There was one thing both women began to desire though.
Although they thought most men were insensitive and untrustworthy, they wanted not only to have children but to add a worthy man to their marriage. This was the topic of their conversation on that particular day. Having lunch together at Isabella's was a ritual in which Tyranny and Jasmine practiced at least twice a week. Both had very busy schedules but both understood the importance of quality time in a relationship.
These women were unconditionally committed to each other and each did whatever possible to keep the other happy. Their relationship was a verbal agreement to be committed to each other but they viewed it as a 'marriage.' They expressed much affection, even in public by hugging, holding hands, and even with short kisses when they greeted each other or departed. The many men in the restaurant assumed these women were engaged in a lesbian relationship but most of them never hesitated to wink, wave or smile whenever they had an opportunity. The women were used to the flirtatious gestures of the men they came into contact with. Each was somewhat flattered sometimes, yet both women regarded the gestures as being either plain lustful or egotistical acts of manhood intended to gain any opportunity to convert them back to what the men thought these women should be. To Jasmine and Tyranny, their choice of living was in no way a contradiction to their womanhood. They were still women. They were just women who happened to be in love with another woman.
However, for the past few months the gestures of men had become somewhat "applications".

"So are you really serious about having children and bringing a man into this marriage, or are you merely thinking of your career?" Tyranny asked, as she put her glass down.

"Tyranny! Now you know I wouldn't do anything like that.
Though my career is very important to me, I would not engage in something I wasn't comfortable with just for the sake of my job. I also love you too much to impose such a thing on you if I knew you weren't totally okay with it."

"Well, it's not that I wouldn't be comfortable with it because the whole idea actually sounds great to me. I just wouldn't want us to be doing it for the wrong reason."

"Trust me sweetheart, it's not for the wrong reason." Jasmine said softly, as she gently grabbed Tyranny's hand and gazed deep into her eyes.

"Okay, so do you have a particular man in mind?"

"Not exactly, but I thought it was something we could discuss, and figure out a way to go about finding one." Jasmine answered.

"Well, first of all he has to be open-minded and mature enough to handle this marriage."

"I agree. I suggest we also seek out a man who understands that you and I have been together for a good while and we'll sometimes need to be together without him."

"Well don't you think we should at least let him watch if he wants to? I mean he would be our husband who we love, and we don't want to neglect him in such a way." Tyranny asked.

"I can deal with that, even though it does sound kind of kinky. But sometimes, he can watch if he wants to."

"He'll also have to be a good man, who's good with raising children, and who'll remain committed to only us." Tyranny suggested.

"Right. He also has to be financially stable with a fairly good job."

"He doesn't have to be rich, does he? I mean, it may be hard to find a rich man who is also a good committed man."
Tyranny responded with a chuckle.

"No," Jasmine began with a giggle, "but he should at least have a steady income...right?"

"Right. And one more thing," Tyranny began to add, "no minute-man'." she finished, which triggered a burst of laughter between the two.

The best of both worlds is what these women desired, and the best of both worlds it would certainly be. What man in his right mind would not want to be married to two, incredibly beautiful women? Not to mention the fact that both women had lots of money. It should have been easy to find a man to fit the character of the man both women agreed upon...but it was not.
Most of the men the two women ran the idea passed only seemed to dwell on the issue of sex. But the marriage would be a very complex one which would require lots of understanding, compromise, and loyalty. These women were not merely interested in having another sex partner because they could find one anywhere. They were looking for a husband who would further enhance that which was already established. Nevertheless months would go by, and they would still have no luck in regards to finding their husband.

While sitting in the living room of their million dollar condominium, Jasmine and Tyranny once again discussed their unique plan.

"Sweetheart," Jasmine began after sipping her cup of cappuccino, "I believe we may be going about this the wrong way. We have men calling day and night, harassing us at work, and even e-mailing us from other states. I think we should come up with another plan." Jasmine continued while sitting on the couch in her silk pajamas, legs curled up.

"I think so too. I just can't seem to figure out what we should do. We can't put an ad in the paper or anything." Tyranny replied, while sitting in a lounge chair cross legged, wearing a short cut t-shirt and panties, and eating chocolate fudge ice cream straight from the container.

"Maybe we should do what we should have done from the start ... do a non-verbal search. You know like pick a few guys we either work with or see out and just watch them. I don't know, this whole idea seems a lot more complicated than it seemed when we originally spoke about it." Jasmine commented, as she put her empty cup down and let her head fall back on the couch with eyes toward the ceiling.

"I know what you mean. We just have to be patient though sweetheart. We both want this but we don't want to begin to get desperate and rush into anything that we'll both regret." Tyranny advised as she put her ice cream down and moved to massage Jasmine's shoulders and neck.

"Ooh, that feels good. I wonder if we can actually pull this off." Jasmine asked with her eyes closed.

"Are you kidding? Of course we can. We just have to be patient like I said." Tyranny answered. "We've overcome larger obstacles than this." She continued.

Both ladies had faced abundant adversity individually before they met as well as while married. Though Jasmine could handle herself due to a series of self defense classes she had taken, Tyranny was a natural fighter. She had grown up in Brooklyn and could take care of herself very well. There had been a few occasions where the two women had gotten into physical altercations with girls and guys who harassed them about their choice of living. Jasmine was beaten up very badly once while she was out alone. A gang of Latino girls saw her coming out of a lesbian club one night and jumped her. Though she quickly recovered, and healed without any traces of the scars she assumed she would have on her face, the incident provoked her to take the classes.
Prior to that incident, she had never been in a fight in her life and actually never anticipated it. However the unfortunate experience at the club dosed her with a reality that she needed to learn how to better defend herself. Jasmine grew up in a Milwaukee suburb as the adopted daughter of a biracial husband and wife attorney team who owned their own firm ... Ambrose and Ambrose. Her life had been fairly protected, attending private schools, then to an Ivy League College, ultimately moving into a successful career.
She was always acknowledged for being the prettiest and most

popular girl at school even though she attended predominantly white schools. In spite of the fact, she never abandoned her blackness … meaning she refused to deny who she was like many blacks in her position had done. People who grow up in other cultures tend to abandon their own identity and take on the identity of those around them. Jasmine refused to do that. She was a black girl in a predominantly white world. That was her reality, yet she had no desire to be white. She did in fact date a white guy once, and though she highly respected her parents. relationship, she did not feel comfortable with engaging in such a relationship herself.

Jasmine remained a virgin until she landed her first job as an intern on Wall Street. A relationship developed between herself and her boss, who was a very yuppie black man who also turned out to be married. She was not in love with him but she had lost her virginity to him, and was devastated when she found out about his wife. Later, she would admit the relationship with her boss and discovering he was married was not quite as serious as it seemed at the time. It was just that the news had come around the same time she discovered she was adopted.

During a visit home one summer, Jasmine stumbled upon letters, and other legal documents which stirred her suspicion. After questioning her parents, she found out that she was in fact adopted. Out of curiosity, she did research to find her real parents. Unfortunately she uncovered the fact that both were deceased, which is why she was put up for adoption in the first place. Feelings of betrayal consumed her. She felt betrayed by her biological parents for passing, her adopted parents for not telling her the truth, and her first physical lover who manipulated her into sleeping with him by promising a long term relationship. She also felt betrayed by the world for its coldness and its selfish ability to unload so much weight on her precious 24 year old mind … a mind which was already so confused about her sexuality. As a result of the overwhelming episodes in her life at the time, she contemplated suicide. Fortunately she met Tyranny in a downtown New York City bar, which was down the street from an exotic dance club Tyranny worked at. Her life and her outlook on life were changed forever.

Tyranny, on the other hand grew up near a housing project in Brooklyn, NY. Her parents were not very rich but they did live comfortably, until her dad died from a heart attack while preaching his Sunday morning sermon. He was the founder of a small Baptist church not far from where she and her family resided. Tyranny's whole life, up until the time her dad died when she was 14 years old, revolved around church. But that Sunday morning when her dad's heart attack was mistaken for the Holy Ghost, and no one called an ambulance until it was too late, she was turned completely away from the faith. She began using drugs heavily, specifically marijuana, and searched for the fatherly love she was missing. Sadly she found it in older men who took advantage of her sexually.

Tyranny ran away from home when she was sixteen, and prostituted herself for money, food, or a place to stay. Sex with men had become nothing more than a means of survival. She was lonely, and in need of affection. And since she found none with men, she began to experiment with lesbian relationships. When she was eighteen years old, she met an older black woman named Cookie who sold drugs. Cookie was abusive at times but Tyranny accepted it not only because the love and affection heavily outweighed the abuse but she had a place to live and drugs whenever she wanted them. Cookie would often take Tyranny to a club which featured female strippers and exotic dancers. Noticing how intrigued Tyranny was by the dancers, Cookie suggested she apply for a position. Tyranny declined because she knew dancing was not all many of the customers expected. Though she could definitely dance, had the body for it, and a pretty face to match, Tyranny really did not want to have sex for money anymore. In the past she had been hurt so badly during sex she would be bleeding and could barely walk. She had no desire to do that anymore. Sex with Cookie never hurt, even when Cookie would use a vibrator or dildo on her. Though she still had a desire to be with men, she did not want to be brutalized.

Years later, though, after Cookie was arrested on drug charges, Tyranny would basically be forced to take a job dancing. She did not know how to do anything else, nor did she have any formal education. That would change once she started dancing. She'd take day classes through which she would acquire a G.E.D., then later complete a 2 year business course which would be the tool she used to achieve success.

Tyranny and Jasmine dated for nearly a year before they ever even kissed. Though Jasmine felt very comfortable being with Tyranny, and was very attracted to her, she was afraid to have sex with her considering she still was not sure about her sexuality. Tyranny never pushed too hard because she recognized Jasmine's fear. Jasmine would later admit that it was the kindness, gentleness and patience with which Tyranny had, that caused her to finally realize being with Tyranny was where she truly wanted to be. After a very strong and loving 4 years together, a job offer for Jasmine moved them to Los Angeles California where Tyranny began her new business. It was then when the two decided to .marry.. From the beginning, Jasmine's parents were supportive of her decision. I guess it was the guilt of her being adopted. Tyranny on the other hand had not seen her mother since she left home. She equated the fact of her mother not looking for her, with the fact that she obviously did not love her. Tyranny was always closer to her father anyway, and when he went away, so did she.

Chapter
2

"All I'm asking, Wil ... are we going to promote her or not? She's been asking about the delay and I'm running out of excuses." Pinkem asked.

"Well Pinkem, you know as well as I do, if we don't promote her she'll most certainly leave the corporation. You also know there is no way in hell I'm going to allow that. Jasmine Ambrose has been one of the best things to happen to this corporation, which means we'd be fools to let her go due to her own personal choice of living." Wil replied.

"But Wil...it is immoral, and could cost us in the future." Pinkem stated.

"Cost us! Cost us what? When it comes to making money, there is no such word as morality. All of our clients come to us to increase their financial status, not educate them on morality! Jasmine Ambrose has made this corporation millions of dollars. Her talent to make our clients money is impeccable, almost mystical even...as if she has a psychic power to locate the most profitable investments. Yes! Jasmine Ambrose will be promoted to senior VP." Wil explained.

"I think you may be making a mistake Wil. Many of our clients pride themselves on the good old-fashioned American way of doing business. And there is nothing American about lesbianism." Pinkem said.
"Pinkem, where have you been for the past decade? Some of entertainments most prominent faces belong to lesbians. World renowned athletes, international business owners, the list goes on. All things considered, I don't honestly believe people really care about another person's sexuality unless it's personal. Also, how can you, a black man, be so inclined to deny a person a better career opportunity due to who they are? Old-fashioned American business has never had anything to do with morality...it was then as it is now...all about money! So stop with

the moral bullshit! Your main reason for not wanting to promote this woman is because of your ego." Wil pointed out.

"Wil that's ridiculous!" Pinkem exclaimed.

"Is it? Everyone knows your despising this woman has to do with the fact that you couldn't get her in bed...which was totally unprofessional and also, might I add, could have cost us a sexual harassment law suit." Wil said.

"But that..." Pinkem began.

"But nothing, you are one of this corporation's top executives, and most times I respect your opinion. Not now though. Jasmine Ambrose will be promoted and that's that! The announcement will be made at the corporation's annual ball." Wil declared.

Abraham Pinkem III is the vice president of the entire Investicom Corporation. He had been one of the corporation's very first employees 22 years prior when the company was founded. His father was a co-founder but died in a plane crash several years after the company began to gain prestige. Pinkem III basically climbed the cooperate ladder to vice president with very little effort, and may unfortunately one day run the cooperation.

Wil Henderson is the president of Investicom, and for the previous 22 years had devoted his life to making it the success it was at present. Wil was a former mill worker from Ohio who, with the help of his best friend Abraham Pinkem II, founded Investicom. He never married, never had any children of his own, and though be basically raised Pinkem III in the business world, he was very worried about the fate of the corporation. After he would no longer be competent enough to run Investicom he may have to turn it over to Pinkem III, unless he could figure out a way to move his favorite employee up in the ranks. Though he was only in his early 60's, his health was beginning to fade due to the damage the mill work had done to his body, and was beginning to manifest itself through slight traces of cancerous tumors on his brain, and frequent chest ailments such as bronchitis. He knew he could not run the corporation for much longer, and unless he could come up with a good plan soon, his irresponsible sex crazed VP would take over.

The Investicom Annual Ball was a very ritzy affair whose guests included not only the top employees of the year but very prestigious clients as well. Jasmine Ambrose was a guest at the ball every year, excluding her first, since she had been employed at Investicom. The only reason she had not made the list then was due to the fact she had only been employed there a few months prior to the ball that year. She loved the affairs, and though she and Tyranny were stared at the entire time, she regarded most of the stares as being ones of admiration. The gowns she and Tyranny wore were always stunning to say the very least. The two women were like celebrities at the balls, and they enjoyed every minute of it.

Tyranny, unlike Jasmine, loved to flirt and be flirted with...as long as there was no touching. Over the years, she had received her share of marriage proposals and even sex proposals from men and women. She was someone to be desired though, not had by anyone except her partner, which is why Jasmine never minded because she knew Tyranny loved her too much to be unfaithful. They had an understanding like no other couple, bisexual or otherwise.

There had been no talk of Jasmine's promotion and she was growing impatient. The promotion had already been delayed for nearly 4 months. She could get no straight answers as to why but she was informed of a meeting that would be held where her promotion would be discussed. The only problem was that the meeting was scheduled a few days after the annual ball, which was upsetting to Jasmine. It was at the ball where promotions were most times announced and she had hoped hers would be amongst the names of those promoted. Apparently it would not happen for her this year. Because the meeting to discuss her promotion was scheduled after the ball, Jasmine began to assume she would not get it.

"I can't believe those assholes aren't going to promote me. I have worked hard for that damned corporation but because I don't live according to their standards, I have to be denied advancement. I have a good mind to not only quit but file a discrimination law suit." Jasmine said angrily as she sat soaking in a hot bubble bath.

"Sweetheart you know I support you in whatever you do, and I understand how angry you are but you may still be promoted. All of the awards and commendations you've gotten prove how valuable you are at Investicom. Maybe you'll still get the promotion, just after the ball." Tyranny explained while sitting on the side of the bathtub and stroking Jasmine's hair.

"That would be just as bad as not getting it at all. Giving me a promotion but keeping it discreet would be insulting! All of my promotions have been discreet, and I'm tired of it! I go to the ball every year watching others being openly promoted and congratulated by all. I have longed to be respectfully acknowledged in such a way. Maybe my work is not as appreciated as I thought." Jasmine said sadly.

"Jasmine don't talk like that sweetheart!" Tyranny exclaimed.

"No it's obvious, and I think it's time I begin to consider some of the offers from other corporations I.ve been getting. Maybe once I'm gone Investicom will understand how costly neglecting employees can be." Jasmine said, as she sank down deeper into the bubbles with a blank stare.

For the previous few years, Jasmine had received very generous offers from a variety of other investment corporations. However, due to her loyalty to Wil, who always respected her regardless of her lifestyle, she declined to accept any. Her career was no longer based primarily on financial status because she had plenty of money. Her focus now was corporate standing.
She understood that though she had achieved much success as an investment broker, there was still a lot she had to learn. Her goal was to one day to own her own firm, and the higher she climbed the ladder, the more she'd learn...which would contribute to the success of the firm she had one day planned to own.

A week had passed with no mention of a promotion, and it was now the night of the ball. Jasmine had considered not even going this year but with Tyranny's persuasion she would not give anyone the pleasure of knowing she was hurt. She also had a plan which would certainly strike a serious blow to Investicom. If she would not be standing in front of that podium receiving a promotion, then she would be standing there announcing her decision to leave the corporation. Several companies were already laying in wait for Jasmine's formal resignation, and a decision on who she would work for. It was not long before Wil got wind of Jasmine's plan, at which time he immediately called her to his office.

"Jasmine!" Wil began in a cheerful way as she stepped into his office. "Come on in and have a seat...we need to talk." He continued.

"Yes, we most certainly do. For eight years I.ve worked my ass off for this damned company! I have been exposed to the most disrespectful and annoying acts of ignorance, yet I've remained loyal...especially to you! I would have never in my wildest dreams imagined that you, of all people, would so blatantly neglect me that which you and everyone else in this firm know I deserve. How could you, Wil? How could you?" Jasmine exclaimed angrily as tears began to flood her eyes.

"Jasmine," Wil began softly, "I'm sorry. Please believe me. I know how valuable an asset you.ve been to this company and me. Your marriage has never been important to me and you know that. You're more than just an employee to me, and I'm damned proud of you and your outstanding work here, which is why I called you in here today. I've heard about your decision to leave us and I was hoping I could persuade you to reconsider." Wil explained.

"No Wil, it's obvious that I'm no longer appreciated around here so I'd rather not be here. Everything else I can take but you turning your back on me is overwhelmingly painful. You once told me you loved me like a daughter and I believed you. But now, I no longer feel comfortable here...so I'm leaving." Jasmine said as she lightly dabbed the moisture from her eyelashes with a tissue she retrieved from Wil's desk.

"Jasmine, if I have ever been anything in my life it is certainly not a liar. I have always been totally honest with you and..." Wil said before being interrupted.

"Totally honest up until now, right? The fallacy is crystal clear. This so called delay in promoting me is merely a smoke screen for you to try to figure out how to deny me." Jasmine pointed out.

"You're almost right Jasmine. True, I have been pussyfooting around as far as your promotion, excuse my French. But guess what!?! I'm not supposed to be telling you this but waiting any longer may cost me a valuable employee. The meeting to discuss your promotion was purposely scheduled after the ball because we didn't want you to make any hasty decisions before then. Apparently we were wrong but I'm sure you'll be glad to know a decision for your promotion has already been made." Wil said as he reached into his desk drawer to retrieve a gold desk top name plate. "Congratulations Ms. Senior VP." He continued while passing the name plate to Jasmine.

"Oh Wil!" Jasmine said as she stared at her chiseled name with the initials S.V.P. next to it.

"I got it for you last week. I was going to personally announce your promotion at the annual ball tonight. So even though you already know, can you still act surprised." Wil said with a slight smile.

"Yes!" Jasmine said as she went around the desk to hug Wil. "Thank you. You just don't know what this means to me." she continued.

"Yes I do. And there is no need for any thanks...you worked damned hard for this." Wil said.

"I did, didn't I?" Jasmine said while still looking at her nameplate.

"Alright, now get back to work!" Will exclaimed with a slight smirk as he turned his back to Jasmine "And make sure you call those other corporate vultures and explain how you won't be leaving." He continued.

"Yes sir." Jasmine replied as she left the office.

The night of the ball, Jasmine wore a glow of pride which could be seen by all. She was on top of the world, and while standing at the podium to accept her plaque and give her speech, emotions got the best of her. Tears streamed down her face like balls of crystal. And as she retreated back to her table to receive her normal warm congratulating hug from Tyranny, a roar of applause and standing ovations, mostly from clients, filled the entire hall. For the rest of the night, Jasmine shook hands, received hundreds of congratulations, and danced with just about everyone who asked. She had been so caught up in glee that she had not noticed the tall brown and handsome "hunk" of a man quietly admiring her from a corner of the hall while he sophisticatedly sipped from a glass of champagne. It was not until Tyranny noticed him and brought it to Jasmine's attention that they both casually sashayed over to where the man was standing. There seemed to be this instant unexplained attraction to this man by both women. Jasmine had never felt this type of chemistry for a man, and it had been a long time, before she and Jasmine began seeing each other, since Tyranny felt this way. Though they were both still attracted to men, no man had stirred so much warm emotion inside of either of them, and without a word, upon their approaching this man, both women simultaneously gave their hands submissively to him.

"Ladies." The man said in a breathtakingly smooth and deep tone, as he lightly kissed both their hands. "Though I'm flattered by both your company, I must excuse myself for staring in such a way. It's just that I have heard an awful lot about you, Ms. Ambrose, and I.ve had an overwhelming desire to meet you." The man continued.

"Well if you've heard anything bad, they're all lies." Jasmine said with a light seductive giggle.

"Oh, but on the contrary, which is why I was compelled to meet you. I traveled over half way across the country for this ball only because I knew you'd be here." The man said in a confessional type way."

"Well! Now I'm feeling flattered. How far exactly did you come?" Jasmine asked as Tyranny was pulled away by Wil to dance.

"Looking for more flattery huh?" The man said with a gorgeous smile.

"Maybe." Jasmine replied while at the same time trying to fight the Goosebumps she felt coming on which were triggered by this man's smile.

"I guess I can oblige. I've never had a problem with complimenting a woman...especially one as beautiful as you. Let me first start off by explaining myself. My name is Peter Phontane, owner and founder of New Beginnings Youth Development in Atlanta, Georgia. Over the past few years I've made a considerable amount of money through small investments but I've decided I would like to increase my profits by making less but larger investments. It has been rumored that you are somewhat an investment Guru and I'd like to work with you." Peter explained.

"Well Mr. Phontane, I don't know about the Guru part, but I'm sure I can help you locate very satisfactory and very profitable investments. Um, is your wife interested in any type of investing?" Jasmine said in a sly prying type way.

"My wife? Oh I'm not married. Sometimes I think my standards are too high for one single woman to fulfill … not that I'm an unfaithful man. As a matter of fact, that's basically the reason I haven't settled down. I don't want to be tempted by another woman who may possess the characteristics my spouse may not have. Selfish huh?" Peter confessed.

"No, I don't think it's selfish at all. You're just a complex man who probably needs to be involved in a complex relationship." Jasmine said as she gently grabbed Peter's hand. "Would you like to dance?" She continued.

"I'd be honored." Peter answered.

Peter Phontane is a 35-year-old stunningly handsome self-made millionaire who stood about 6.2" and weighed approximately 210 pounds, with a trim and chiseled build. He has a slightly burnt bronze complexion, with short jet black wavy hair and distinct African features. He also had dark brown eyes which shone constantly and had an instant hypnotic effect on women as well as men. He grew up an orphan in Atlanta, and stayed in so much trouble that his destiny seemed to be filled with nothing but despair. Up until the time he was 17 years old, he had been in 3 different group homes and 2 juvenile detention centers. It was apparent he was rebelling due to the fact that no family had ever been interested in adopting him.

Considering his age at the time he was originally placed in the orphanage, it was expected by the administration there that prospective parents would most likely over look him. He was about 3 1/2 years old, and a black male child. Most people during that time, when choosing black children, sought females. Also, prospective parents tend to look for children under the age of 1year old, but will sometimes settle for a 2-year-old due to the transitional aspect of the adoption process. When a child knows his original parents, getting used to a brand new set of parents is difficult.

So with all things considered, Peter, whose name was the same as his father who was named after the Apostle of the Bible, remained in the orphanage until he was 12. He was then transferred to a boy's home. His last name stemmed from a nickname he got as a child, "Fountain." Late nights in the orphanage, Peter would get out of his bed and wander into a hallway area outside of the large room where he and 14 other orphans slept. Early in the morning, when the staff would make their routine checks on the children, they would find Peter sleeping in a sitting position while propped up next to the water fountain which sat in the hallway. As he got older, his creative mind developed the name Phontane. His birth records had all been mysteriously lost, which meant his original last name was unknown. No one knew why Peter never spoke of his sir name, because he was surely old enough at almost 4 years old to know it. Everyone concluded it was obviously the trauma of losing his parents.

At the age of 15, Peter began to realize he would soon be considered an adult and he would have to leave the group home. He thought of what he could do to make it in the world but he could not come up with one single idea. Then it hit him. He had always been good at fixing things. Sometimes he would buy or steal old bikes, fix them up, then sell them. He figured this was a good way to make a little extra money, so he began to read through classified newspapers ads with the intent of finding things he could buy for cheap, then sell for a profit. The counselors at the home began to recognize his potential so they would contribute to helping him buy things to see exactly what he could do. Mostly they would get him old toys, bikes and even small appliances. Then, as he got older, they got him old cars and supplies for him to test his talent. Some of those cars he worked on would turn out to run almost like brand new, and Peter would sell them and share the profit with those who invested money in him.

Peter ultimately moved up to buying abandon properties, renovated, and sold them in order to move on to bigger opportunities ... which ultimately manifested into a successful realty company. Nevertheless, regardless of his success, Peter Phontane never forgot about the unfortunate children and teens who occupy so many orphanages and group homes all over his home state. He showed love to as many as he could. With money he made from his reality company, Peter founded New Beginning Youth Development, which not only educated youth academically but also had vocational type courses which would help to establish or further develop talents, hidden or otherwise, within the youth. Multitudes of youths, who had been involved in his programs, have graduated from college and become small successes themselves. Some also eventually join Peter and his small group of volunteer entrepreneurs who contribute their time and money into helping youth. A total of 3 youth centers and a group home can be accredited to Peter. He did it all for the kids. He loved them, and would adopt every orphan he could if it were possible. Well, in a sense he had. He one day hoped though to have children of his very own, with whom he would show the love from a parent, that he himself was neglected as a child.

Chapter
3

The night at the ball with Peter seemed to temporarily cloud all memory of Jasmine's promotion. Both Jasmine and Tyranny took turns dancing and talking with him for the entire night. It was exhilarating listening to him speak of his love for children and his desire to have a multi versatile woman, after all, what could be more versatile than two women? His positive and unselfish contributions to helping better the lives of others were also impressive, which was another plus in his favor. To them, Peter seemed to be the perfect candidate for a husband but there was one problem. It was not the fact that Peter lived so far away because both women were almost certain he was worthy enough to be trusted to remain committed...even from such a long distance. His character screamed loyalty and commitment. Traveling, considering their financial status, would also certainly not be a problem for any of them; living with them was never a stipulation which Jasmine and Tyranny ever discussed anyway. Separate houses would ensure the fact that they would both have the time each desired to be alone. The problem? Well, though Peter flirted openly with both of them, it was still difficult to determine if he was casually flirting or if his flirting was provoked by intimate interest. Neither woman wanted to come off too strongly considering it may have suggested they were interested in nothing more than a ménage' a trios', which was not even remotely close to what they were truly interested in. This whole situation would have to be approached delicately.

Peter's acceptance of the relationship between Jasmine and Tyranny was clearly apparent when considering not only the kind and unbiased way he treated them but also the comfortable manner through which he openly discussed his personal past. And though they would have both liked to have some sort of sign from him, both women later agreed his lack of aggressiveness further strengthened the level of trust with which they had already begun to develop for this very characteristically rare man.

"You felt it too!" Jasmine exclaimed as both she and Tyranny walked through the front door of their home.

"Jasmine... I can't totally explain what went on tonight but that man was sent here for us." Tyranny said as she walked toward the kitchen.

"It certainly seems that way but as you said before, we'll have to be patient. Maybe develop a close friendship with him, do some things together as a group, and through casual conversation we'll eventually make our proposal. We don't want to chase him away." Jasmine explained as she joined Tyranny in the kitchen for a final toast.

"Everything will work out, I can feel it. But for now, I'd like to once again congratulate you on your promotion Ms. Ambrose." Tyranny said with a raised glass of champagne. "and a toast to complex marriages." She continued.

"Why thank you Ms. Elliot. I second that." Jasmine said with a short giggle as she doused down her drink and moved in closer to Tyranny. "Have I told you how much I love you?" Jasmine continued.

"Yes but how about you show me." Tyranny responded as she wrapped her arms around Jasmine's neck and began to slowly kiss her.

"Come on." Jasmine replied as she took Tyranny's hand and led her to the bedroom.

Jasmine and Tyranny made love all night, as they usually did, though not as regularly as most people thought. Their marriage was not based on sex, it was based on the same type of love which most heterosexual marriages are based on. These women were not freaks ... they were two very intelligent and business minded adult women who chose a mate and married that mate. Social acceptance was not a priority nor was it a desire. They lived their lives as best they knew how ... which was just as normal as any other human being. Though they did engage in lots of non-sexual intimacy such as kissing and touching and other things of the sort, it was merely showing a healthy amount of appreciation for their spouse, which contributes to the strength and stability of the marriage. A lot of couples could learn a thing or two from these women.

Back at Investicom, things were about as hectic as Jasmine had briefly anticipated on her way to work that morning. There were whispers, cold stares, and though it had been a while since Jasmine found any surprises in her desk, on this morning she found an artificial vagina known as a "Fifi" with a pair of false teeth stuffed inside.

"Creative." Jasmine said out loud as she held up the insulting and uncouth surprise.

She made it a practice to expect such things from her co-workers, which made it easy to avoid being bothered by them. Despite the fact that she never gave any of her secret pranksters the pleasure of knowing they hurt her ... she was human, and some of the pranks hit her deep. There had been a few occasions when she actually went in the restroom at work and cried. She clearly understood the prejudice imposed on gays and lesbians in this society but it was hard to swallow. How could adults be so cruel?

Jasmine was a kind, compassionate, gentle, and thoughtful woman. There were more than a few times when she had ordered take out lunch for her whole department, and paid out of her own pocket. She gave anonymous Christmas gifts, flowers and candy on Valentine's Day, cards and small gifts for the mothers and fathers in her department on their perspective days and never asked for anything in return. She never even let it be known that she gave the gifts because, not only was secrecy more exciting and special, she did not want to be offended by the gifts being given back.

Jasmine also volunteered time at soup kitchens and gave anonymous checks to different charities. She was a wonderful human who had never said or done anything bad to anyone who did not deserve it. Yet and still, she was being unjustifiably tormented by jealous women and men whose proposals to sleep with her were denied. Even when the proposals were offensively laid out, she still remained calm and kind in her denial. A lot of men in her department, and some she knew outside her job, viewed her being 'lesbian' as a strike to their egos. But she did not label herself lesbian, she preferred bisexual, and her choice of living had nothing to do with anyone but herself and Tyranny.

On this particular day, Jasmine ignored the childishness. Nothing was going to spoil her day in light of the fact that she had enjoyed a wonderful night of great sex with her spouse, with whom she would also be having one of their regular luncheons at Isabella's. She also had beautiful anticipations of her and Tyranny's potential futures with Peter Phontane. She could not help but remember his strong hands and the firm but comfortable grip with which he held her when they danced. She could not forget those lovely attentive brown eyes that focused totally on herself or Tyranny as either of them spoke, the smooth way he danced, his short wavy black hair, the strength in his strong looking face, and his trim hard muscular body with definition so deep … she could feel the detail even through his tailor made Italian suit as they danced. The emotion he aroused in her was something she could not escape. Even as she thought about him she could feel her blood racing with excitement… not to mention the moisture between her legs. Yet she did not feel the least bit guilty about her thoughts because her commitment to Tyranny was certainly not in jeopardy.

Jasmine, after retreating to her office at the back of the department, quickly turned on her desk fan and sat directly in front of it in an attempt to cool off and regain her composure. She considered smoking one of her Newport light cigarettes, as she occasionally did when at work but before she could get the pack out of her desk drawer, her secretary's voice came over the intercom.

"Yes." Jasmine responded.

"Ms. Ambrose, there is a Mr. Peter Phontane here to see you. He says he has an appointment." The secretary stated.

"Thank you. Send him in." Jasmine responded.

She then quickly began fixing her hair and clothes, checked her make-up, and turned the fan on high!

"Come in." Jasmine said in response to a knock on her door.

"Ms. Ambrose." Peter said as he stuck his head inside the door.

"Hi Mr. Phontane, come on in." Jasmine said with a hard smile as she got up to greet Peter.

"I hope you didn't forget our appointment for today. I'll be heading back to Atlanta in a few hours and I wanted to discuss some things before I go." Peter explained.

"Oh. You.re going back already?" Jasmine asked in a disappointed sort of way.

"Yes, I have some other business to take care of. I'm also doing something with the kids. If things sound good though, visiting LA could become a frequent practice." Peter said.

"I assume 'things' is in reference to profit?" Jasmine asked.

"Well yes. What else would I be talking about?" Peter responded.

"I mean though making money is great, there are other important aspects to life." Jasmine pointed out.

"Ms. Ambrose, for the record, though making money is very important to me, it in no way infers that I am a greedy man. I am in a position where I need currency to fulfill the obligations I have to my kids." Peter pointed out.

"Excuse me for the misunderstanding, I was in no way suggesting that you were greedy...I apologize. It's just that Tyranny and I..." Jasmine began before she wisely caught herself.

"Tyranny and you what?" Peter asked with a curious look on his face.

"Never mind, let's just get back to the business at hand." Jasmine said as she began getting out stock reports and other investment information to show Peter.

During the whole meeting with Peter, Jasmine was distracted. Though Peter did not actually notice due to Jasmine's high level of discipline and professionalism, she knew eventually she would have to come up with a mature and tasteful way to make the proposal to Peter that she and Tyranny had discussed.

"Patience," she kept thinking to herself, "patience."

At about this same time, Tyranny was on her job going over some figures in her books, and looking through brochures for a new line of beauty products which would soon be hitting the market. Considering the prestige of her businesses, as well as the clientele, she usually received information on new products long before other smaller salons did. And though she had her own office in each of her salons, she opted to look over paperwork or brochures in the midst of her clients. It was easier to discover how to better cater to their needs. She took her work very seriously and understood how important it was for her to keep her clients satisfied...which she consistently did.

Tyranny did not face the same type of ridicule at her job as Jasmine did but there were still remarks, some sly and others ignorant, with which she patiently but firmly dealt with. On this particular day, while sitting in front of the large front window of one of her salons, a fairly handsome man, who looked to be in his early twenties walked into her salon? The man waved at a woman who was getting a perm, and then he sat down and began flipping through a magazine. Apparently he was waiting for the woman with whom he waved. The man was receiving a lot of non verbal attention from many of the women in the salon, especially an early 40's employee named Valerie, who always had a problem with keeping her thoughts to herself, and was compelled to voice them to Tyranny.

"Ooh girl ... that young man is so fine. The things I could do with that young stud. Whew ... I'm getting hot just thinking about it. What do you think about him girl?" Val asked.

"He's all right I guess." Tyranny said after only quickly glancing at the man, then focusing her attention back to the brochures.

"Oh. I didn't mean to offend you. I forgot about you um ... you know?" Val explained.

"No I don't know Val. You forgot what? That I like women?" Tyranny boldly asked as she looked up at Val with a smile.

"Tyranny ... I didn't mean to be rude." Val humbly explained.

"I'm sure you didn't. But let me explain something to you. Yes ... I do love Jasmine, and I'd never do anything to hurt her, nor would I ever be unfaithful. But just because I'm married to a woman doesn't mean I don't recognize attractive men ...O.K.? So please stop considering me some type of non human creature." Tyranny boldly explained.

This was basically why Tyranny was not hassled as much as Jasmine because Tyranny was more vocal when people disrespected her, or Jasmine. She would also be willing to fight if her words were not enough to alleviate the problem. Not that she was a wild woman or anything, she just settled for nothing less than total respect. Jasmine, too, wanted respect but she chose to go the alternative route…usually just keeping things to herself. Tyranny would explain to Jasmine how it was unhealthy but Jasmine was set in her ways. She was not the type of person who wanted to hurt other people's feelings…even if they hurt hers.

Also on this day, Tyranny too was experiencing post emotional symptoms from the previous night with Peter. Just the thought of him made her heart beat faster. Her thoughts of Jasmine were also strong. She concluded from her conversation with Jasmine the previous evening, Jasmine was feeling things which she had not ever sincerely felt for a man before. Though she knew Jasmine was attracted to some men, the feelings were not as extreme as they were for Peter, and Tyranny was wondering how Jasmine was coping. Tyranny knew what it was like to feel so strongly for a man because she herself was fanatically in love with a man once. It was before she met Cookie, her very first serious relationship with a woman. "The man", which was how Tyranny spoke of him, broke her heart with his cheating. He knew how much Tyranny loved him, which is why he treated her the way he did but she was never a dummy, and it did not take her long to figure out leaving him would certainly be best for her. She would pick up the pieces of her broken heart and take them elsewhere to put them back together. Anyway, Tyranny decided to call Jasmine to see how she was holding up.

"Ms. Ambrose, you have a call on line one." The secretary's voice said over the intercom.

"Who is it?" Jasmine politely asked.

"It's Ms. Elliot." The secretary replied.

"Thank you. Put her through, please." Jasmine said. "Hi Sweetheart." She continued lightly into the phone after being connected."

"Hi. How are you holding up." Tyranny asked.

"Holding up? Well, I'm doing fine I guess but why would you ask that?" Jasmine replied.

"I was just thinking about Peter and..." Tyranny began.

"Oh. I know what you mean now. Well I was a little heat struck earlier when he was here." Jasmine said in a sort of boastful way.

"He was there?" Tyranny exclaimed.

"Yes, he came to discuss business though." Jasmine said.

"So, what now?" Tyranny asked.

"Well things went fairly well and he liked a lot of my suggestions. He'll be coming back to LA in a week or two so we can begin putting things in motion." Jasmine explained.

"Back to LA?" Tyranny asked.

"Yes. He had some business to take care of in Atlanta, so he had to fly out today. But he will be back." Jasmine answered.

"That's good to know. I wish I could have gotten an opportunity to see him before he left, but oh well. And since I know you're alright, I'm going to get back to work O.K.? I love you...and I'll see you for lunch." Tyranny said.

"O.K. I love you, and I can't wait." Jasmine replied as they both hung up the phone.

Chapter
4

In a small dank one-room apartment, a woman in her mid fifties sits staring out of her dingy window with her thick salt and pepper hair pulled back in a bun and covered with a hair net. In her slightly coffee stained uniform tightly fitting, legs crossed, and hands laid in her lap, she sits in an old raggedy sofa lounge chair with her weary blood shot brown eyes observing every single person who walked by on the street below. Pimps, pushers, prostitutes, peddlers, and police...everything and everybody who moved or walked by- she watched. It had been approximately thirty years since her last glimpse, and even though she would not know when she saw whatever or whoever it was which she had searched for so long, hope was the only thing that kept her alive...if that's what you want to call it.

It had been a little over 3 months since Margaret last mustered up the strength to clean her apartment. Her strength came only in very moderate and periodic spurts. The air in that apartment was dusty and dry, almost enough to suffocate a person, with a smell which was a mixture of mildew, body odor, and mothballs. Sometimes she would sit for days, caught up in her own thoughts, gazing out of that window only to be brought back by a knock at her door. Most times it would be either the big burly, scraggly bearded landlord coming to collect the $350 a month rent, or one of her employees coming to check on her and to remind her of the fact that she had to work. It was fully understood by many just what the woman was going through. Everyone who was aware of her burdensome past sympathized with her. Her employer was extremely patient with her too. She would have occasional fainting spells where she would just fall out while working and have to sit for 20 to 30 minutes before she could get back on her feet. And though she was only 52 years old, her appearance caused most people to regard her as a very elderly woman.

Ever since her husband of only 2 years died 32 years prior of pneumonia, her life had been horribly miserable. At only 20 years old at the time Margaret was faced with a life which would crucify her soul. She herself was stricken with a serious illness shortly after her husband's death, and was lucky to have lived through it. Sometimes she wished she had died because as a result of the illness, she was forced to give up her most precious possessions. And due to circumstances beyond her control, along with a lack of money and a hospital bill which would take her nearly ten years to pay off, retrieving her possessions became virtually impossible. Occasionally she would get recurring disappointing letters which basically said "no luck," that she would put in a drawer with the many other "no luck" letters. Afterward she would then drift back into her immobilizing state of misery. Tears had not fallen from her eyes in over a decade though she used to cry all of the time. Now the painful fire which burned inside was no longer quenched. Her well was dry. There were no more tears. Nothing left but an ever-burning fire inside which imprisoned her soul in a living hell.

Her name was Margaret Simmons-Buckley. She was born and raised in a small Alabama town called Prattville, the tenth of 13 children who grew up very poor in a small 2 room wooden house. Slavery no longer existed in the south during that time but blacks were still treated cruelly and denied many job opportunities. Cotton picking, hay bailing, and other farm labor jobs were basically the only jobs blacks had no problems getting. And by the time she was 6 years old- Margaret, both her parents, and nine of her brothers and sisters were working together in cotton fields. Though her parents were surprisingly loving, considering their situation, and instilled not only a sense of family unity but religious values in all of their children...Margaret despised her life, resented her family, and hated picking cotton or any other labor which was abundantly piled on her and her family. She longed to get out of that house, away from her suffering family, and out of Alabama.

By the time Margaret was barely 17, most of her older brothers and sisters had run away from home, and her parents had began slowly deteriorating from the many decades of hard labor they had done in their lives. This meant they could not do as much work, basically boiling down to the fact that the children would have to pick up the slack. Yet with only 5 children left at home...the work was hard. So much pressure ultimately prompted Margaret to run away with a boy, Peter Buckley, who she had been seeing secretly since she was barely in her teens. He lived not far from where she did, and late at night they would meet in a wooded area near both their homes. During one of their midnight rendezvous, they decided to run away to North Carolina to get married. They settled in Asheville, North Carolina, where Peter died only 2 years later.

It had been 2 days since Margaret had been out of her apartment. She had neither bathed nor taken off her work clothes. There was a half-eaten ham sandwich, which had begun to mold, and a full glass of water in a dirty glass sitting on an end table which sat next to Margaret. She grew up in a good family. Though she did run away, her family was very close knit, instilled a certain extent of family value, and stressed the desire to fulfill family obligations.

Margaret's running away had nothing to do with a loss of love for her family. Her desire to run stemmed from the dissatisfaction she felt over a good family working so hard to reap no better prosperity than poverty. And because her personal obligations changed, it had come time for her to start thinking of herself and her future family. She did not want the same for her unborn son. But how could she have done such a thing. It was not the way she was brought up and she agonized over it. She was tormented all of her life as punishment for what she considered an unforgivable deed. What else could she have done though? Her life had taken a drastic change for the worse. She basically had no other choice.

Workers at Freddie's Diner, which was where Margaret worked, recognized the misery overwhelming Margaret and offered a considerable amount of support. Pity, along with the fact that even with her lack of communication Margaret was a kind and gentle woman, caused some of the workers to look out for her. On days when her thoughts had her trapped in a world not comprehended by others, Margaret sometimes forgot to go to work. She had no phone at her apartment but she lived only a block or two from Freddie's. Coworkers would go to Margaret's place in hopes of getting her to go in for at least a shift. Most times she would return to work with them. Other times though, she would be too depressed to even get up and answer the door. Whoever may have been the one to go check on Margaret, after getting no answer at the door, would go down to the street and look up to see Margaret sitting and staring out the window. Seeing her would at least verify the fact that she was alive ... physically at least.

On one particular morning, a young woman in her early thirties named Angie, knocked on Margaret's door. She worked with Margaret and was one of the workers who regularly checked on her.

"Ms. Margaret. Are you in there? You know it's time for you to work. It's a nice day outside too. You don't wanna miss all the sunshine. You got some mail out here." Angie said through the door as she lightly knocked. A few minutes passed before the clicking of a lock being unlocked sounded from the other side of the door. The door opened and Margaret was standing in her dingy uniform with a sweater slung over one arm and a small tote bag, which held only an umbrella and a bible, hanging on the other.

"Are you doing okay Ms. Margaret?" Angie asked as she handed Margaret her mail.

"Yes." Margaret answered with an emotionless expression on her face as she took the pieces of mail, and began opening them. There was one particular letter Margaret focused most of her attention. After glancing over the letter, Margaret looked back up at Angie with a smile and continued,

"I'm doing just fine."

Angie was a short, "big boned" cocoa brown complexioned woman who was devoted to the Baptist church. She had a cute face with pretty white teeth which surrounded a small gap in between her top front two. Her eyes were dark brown and she wore a small diamond nose ring. She was always very pleasant even though she had somewhat of a dramatic life of her own. Her parents had died years earlier, she had no brothers or sisters and her husband was an alcoholic. But she kept her faith in God.

Angie was never used to seeing Margaret smile with her teeth showing. Most times Margaret's smile was extremely slight and barely noticeable. So the brightness in Margaret's face on thisday was a surprise.

"You got some good news Ms. Margaret?" Angie asked.

"Yes," Margaret began, "very good news!" She continued as she handed Angie the letter. The letter was a usual telegram which Margaret periodically received, and it read:

Mrs. Buckley,

We may have a lead. It is imperative that I see you in order to discuss the steps that will be further taken. Please come to my office as soon as possible.

Detective Archibald

"That is good news Ms. Margaret. I guess you had better get yourself together and catch a bus downtown. Come on." Angie said as she gently took Margaret by the arm and went back inside the apartment.

Once inside, Angie helped Margaret bathe and get dressed. She then took Margaret outside to a bus stop and put her on a bus headed for town. Margaret already knew what bus to get on and where to get off…she had done it many times before. But Angie, caring a lot for Margaret, made sure the bus driver knew where he should let Margaret off. She always made sure to look out for Margaret.
Ever since she had known her, Angie regarded Margaret as a sort of motherly figure. They never talked about mother-daughter things, and only spent time together mostly at work, however there was an unspoken love between the two. They occasionally went to church together, though Margaret's faith had wavered over the years. She could not understand Gods way. It was this lack of understanding that caused her to believe God was in some way letting her down. What had she done to deserve so much pain? She read the bible and prayed even when she did not even realize it but still could not understand why her life was so mercilessly taken away. Maybe it was because she abandoned her parents and younger siblings. Who knew? Hopefully the news she had gotten in that telegram was an indication of the fact that God was bestowing a little mercy… finally.

Chapter

5

"I came ta' bring the pain, hard core from the brain." A tall skinny black teen yells as he runs back down the basketball court after dunking the basketball, "Ya'll can't stop me...I'm the mothafuckin' man." He continued.

His name is Terrell "Taz" Buckley, a local kid who belonged to one of Peter's youth groups. A few months prior, Taz was found lying in an alley near one of the centers in the city bleeding profusely from 3 bullet wounds to the chest and mid section. He was only 15 years old at the time but belonged to a local gang called the "A.T.L. Mobsters."

Apparently, he had been caught in the alley by what was believed to have been a rival gang, shot, and left for dead. Several other teenagers, who were on their way to the youth center in the city saw Taz in the alley on the ground and immediately ran to inform Peter. Peter, along with a few other counselors from the center, put Taz in one of the center's vans and took him to the hospital. Taz was unconscious when they found him and his pulling through was doubtful. But he did...with Peter, who had been checking on him daily, standing close by.

"How are you feeling young man?" Peter asked while standing next to the hospital bed Taz occupied.

"I'm cool. But look man...Just like I told those other detectives...I don't know who shot me." Taz said as he turned his gaze from Peter to the television where cartoons were playing.

"I'm not a detective young brother. My name is Peter and I run a youth center not far from where you were shot. The police told me you didn't have any family and..." Peter began before being interrupted by Taz.

"What you mean? I got family! A.T.L. Mobsters is my family. They gon' be comin' ta' get me in a few, as soon as they find out where I'm at." Taz said half angrily.

"Well brother, you.ve been here for 5 days already and no one has asked about you, nor has anyone come to visit." Peter explained.

"Five days? You lyin'!" Taz exclaimed.

"When you woke up this morning, you were waking up from a 5 day rest. Don't you find it strange that you're watching Saturday morning cartoons and you were shot on Monday?" Peter pointed out.

"Well, my boys just don't know where I'm at that's all." Taz replied in an attempt to fool even himself into believing he had not been abandoned.

"That's not true and I think you know it. The police saw that "mobsters" tattoo on your chest and they questioned some of them about the shooting. They claimed to not even know you. What did you do man? Why did your own crew try to kill you?" Peter asked.

"Man you crazy. My boys wouldn't do no shit like that." Taz answered without looking at Peter.

"Then why did they claim not to know you? And why won't you tell the police who shot you?" Peter asked.

Taz answered only with silence.

"You told the police they wore masks but you know who they were don't you?" Peter asked.

Taz still remained silent. Tears began to stream uncontrollably from the corners of his eyes down to his ears. His lips trembled as he tried to speak but emotions overwhelmed him and all he could do was cry. Peter in turn grabbed Taz's hand from his face and said

"Don't worry brother...I've got your back."
After Taz was released from the hospital, in Peter's custody of course, he was taken to a group home outside of the city which Peter also founded. It was basically a large ranch house which sat on a little over 5 acres of land. There were a few cows,

41

chickens, roosters and goats. There was also a large vegetable garden and some fruit trees. The upkeep of the animals and the garden was the responsibility of the youth who were housed there. Most of the kids were ex gang members, teen prostitutes, or other youth who were on the wrong paths.

The purpose of this particular group home was to serve as a sort of fresh start for youth who had not had a fair shake in life. Peter felt a deep compassion for all human beings but more so for youth. He himself had experienced the cruelty with which society imposed on its less fortunate youth but still he turned out to be a success. He had hoped he could in some way contribute to the success of others who were facing that which he had overcome. Though the youth had lots of responsibilities, there was always time set aside for recreation or other personnel time with which the teens could do their own thing. They were all still basically kids, and Peter did not want them to miss out on that phase of their lives.

As Taz ran to the other end of the court, his baggy black sweat shorts bounced side to side as if there was no one in them. He was very skinny but a tower for his age. Though he was only now 16, he stood 6'6" and a half. He wore no shirt showing off his bony and now tattoo-less chest. The removal of all gang related tattoos was a requirement which none of the group members opposed to. They were at the home to change their lives, which meant all of their negative past had to be left behind. Taz also wore a pair of Michael Jordan sneakers, which were sort of an incentive gift, from Peter, for Taz to join the group. He loved basketball and has unbelievable talent on the court.

"Firs' you wanna be like mike, now you wanna be like Tupac!" A young Hispanic girl, named Lena, yelled from the bleachers.

"Yeah well singin' lyrics don't make him no Tupac...O-kay." A young black girl named Rochelle, who was sitting nearby, pointed out while rolling her eyes in a sassy gesture.

"I heard that." Lena replied with a slight chuckle while stomping her foot.

"Why ya'll wanna talk about a brotha'! Let Pac rest in peace." A young Korean boy said.

"Pac ain't dead!" Taz screamed as he blocked a shot attempt, made by another youth on the court, with so much force the ball sailed over the heads of the youth watching from the bleachers. A loud

"ooohhh..." filled the air followed by the sound of feet rhythmically pounding the bleachers.

"This is my mothera' fuckin' house!" Taz exclaimed with his hands held high. "Don't nobody hit shit unless I let 'em." He continued.

"Hey, hey, hey! What's with all the foul language out there?" A counselor named Cassandra Adams exclaimed as she appeared in the doorway of the house.

"Excuse me Ms. Adams. A brotha jus' got a lil hyped." Taz explained.

"Yeah, well try to control yourself, O.K.? God can hear that and I don't think he appreciates it."

"Yes maam." Taz replied with his head hanging down...mostly in an attempt to hide his slight smirk.

"He's laughin. Ms. Adams." Rochelle yelled.

"That's alright. I'll fix him tomorrow come chore time. Then we'll see who'll be laughing." Ms. Adams replied with a slight smirk of her own as she disappeared back inside the house.

Cassandra Adams is a twenty-seven year old black Christian woman who had worked with this particular group for 6 years. She started her career off while still in college as a youth counselor at a public school in Atlanta, and met Peter there at a function proposing an alternative school for trouble youth. After talking personally with Peter, and learning of his dedication to helping youth, she decided to join his crusade. There was no question that she was sincerely concerned with helping youth but her speedy decision to work for him was slightly motivated by her attraction to him as well. He was very handsome and they both shared similar concerns for youth. From the very first day she laid eyes on Peter she had a crush on him. Most women did.

Shortly after her being hired, the two dated casually for a few months but intimate relations never occurred. The chemistry felt by Cassandra was unfortunately not felt by Peter. Though she was a very attractive dark complexioned woman, petite, with an excellently firm shape, and character and brains to match...Peter's uncertainty about the type of woman he needed in his life caused him to limit their relationship to strictly friendship.

After their breakup it had been rumored, not by Cassandra but others who knew of their dating, that Peter may have been gay but there was no evidence to prove this absurd accusation. Peter himself laughed when he was made aware of the rumor and never tried to prove the contrary. He merely carried himself as he usually did. After all, he knew how much he adored women but was man enough to refrain from trying to prove himself to others. He and Cassandra still remain to be the best of friends. And even with the occasional flirting Cassandra may engage, which is basically her way of showing Peter she is still very much interested in him, there has never been an ill moment in their friendship. Well, aside from the time Cassandra proposed the idea of having mandatory religious classes for the youth. She believed a daily dose of the Holy Ghost was exactly what the kids needed. Peter on the other hand, a non-religious yet believer in God, felt as though imposing religion on the kids would complicate his original motive. Of course Cassandra was outraged considering her Christian background and felt as though Peter was wrong in his decision. But after he pointed out how religion was not a bad idea, as long as the individual kids wanted it there was not a problem. He even quoted a scripture which stated "No man can come to the Father unless he is drawn."

Unable to debate a quote from the very book she committed her life to, Cassandra broke her vow of silence toward Peter after 4 whole weeks! Sure, Cassandra was a good woman, humane, and excellent with the kids...whom she loved dearly. However, though Peter would never publicly admit it, it was her extreme outlook on religion that was sort of the wedge driven between his and her intimate relationship.

It was not unusual for Peter to be absent from the home for days at a time because everyone understood he had centers all over the city with which he must oversee. They also understood he was a businessman who had his own company to run as well.

So expecting to see him daily was unheard of. Sometimes, he would call ahead before he visited. Yet other times, loving to be greeted with the overwhelming joy of his kids being surprised, he arrived unannounced, always starting his greeting off with

"I was in the neighborhood so I decided to drop by."

The familiar sound of a honking horn could be heard in the distance. Then, up over the small slope in the road came rolling that shiny black chrome trimmed 1999 Lincoln Navigator, limited edition, with a smiling Peter Phontane in the driver's seat. The kids were used to seeing Peter dressed very casually whenever he visited but on that particular day his green and white Nike sneakers with black bottoms, his white shorts with green lettering spelling Nike on the left, the matching tank top with the Nick symbol on the right side of his chest, along with the two diamond earrings made him look like one of them. Cassandra, on the other had found herself being aroused by Peter's well proportioned muscular build.

His hairy bowed legs seemed to be nothing but expertly shaped masses of muscle. That firm strong looking behind tantalized her to the point where she just wanted to slap it to see if it would shake. And the hairy chest bulging from the sides and top of his tank top made her heart beat like a drum during an African ceremonial festival. He was a black god, and the sight of him made Cassandra blush with weakness.

The other girls, though they stared in awe, kept their comments to themselves until they were alone as a group where they would squawk and giggle and grab themselves in a sort of hug while falling on the bed and screaming about how fine he was and what they would do with a man like him. They were fully aware of Peter's level of manhood and feared that any flirting would not only be inappropriate but also warrant a long painful speech. He was old enough to be most if not all of their father. The guys, though envious, never allowed the envy to cause a dislike for Peter. He was a good guy who loved them and would do anything he possibly could for them. They loved and admired him just the same.

"Hello Cassandra." Peter said after his normal greeting.

"Hello." Cassandra replied with eyes lowered like a schoolgirl.

"Yo Pete, what up wit the gear?" The shit's…I mean stuff is dope but you look like one of us." Taz said while briefly looking over at Cassandra who was staring angrily at him.

"You think so huh?" Peter answered. "Well that's the intent. See I was down at Piedmont Park talking to teens like you all, and I figured I'd be better accepted if I could get them to accept me and feel comfortable with my presence. A good role model is one with whom others can relate. It makes helping them a lot easier." Peter explained.

"You so wise Peter." Lena said in a soft sort of entranced type voice.

"And you so goofy." Taz yelled as he pushed Lena.

"Why don't you stop playin. all the time and be a man." Rochelle said as she pushed Taz back in Lena's defense.

"Yeah, lil boy." Lena said as she rolled her eyes at Taz.

"Taz, chill brother. Don't put your hands on women like that, understand?" Peter said calmly yet forcefully.

"Yeah, my bad Pete." Taz replied.

"So how is everything out here?" Peter asked as he turned toward Cassandra.

"Everything is great. You all go on inside and get cleaned up for dinner." Cassandra said as she briefly turned her attention to the kids.

"Pete, we gon' get at up before you peel out?" Taz asked while walking backward toward the house.

"Yes, I'll be inside in a minute." Peter replied. "So, how is he doing Cassandra?" Peter asked while still staring at Taz as he walked in the house.

"He still hasn't totally opened up yet during our therapy groups but his reading is greatly improving, and he's not complaining about the pains in his chest anymore." Cassandra answered.

"Good. And what about you? Are you doing okay? I mean

you spend all of your time either here or at church functions. What about a social life...you know like dating?" Peter asked while at the same time wishing he had not.

"Peter, the lord provides most of my needs and desires. As far as a physical relationship...you know I long to have that. You also know that there is only one man on this earth with whom my heart truly belongs but due to circumstances I still don't quite understand, I cannot have that man. I am still deeply in love with him, and I will always be for the rest of my life." Cassandra explained while looking deeply into Peter's eyes.

Peter was left virtually speechless. The only thing he could say was

"I hear you."

Cassandra knowing of the uncomfortable situation she had just put Peter in, decided to have mercy.

"I'll let you go this time. Come on inside and have a bite to eat." She said as she gently intertwined her arm in his and led him into the house.

Confusion swept through Peter's mind, followed by an overflow of emotion which was not normal to him. It was at that moment when he began to see just how beautiful Cassandra really was. He realized just how much of a catch she truly was. All of the guys in the youth group were infatuated with her, just as many men who knew her outside of the group. Each always tried to impress her by outdoing the other. The way her body swayed when she walked. Her dark brown "cat eyes" and even her hair, though short, was always appealingly styled simply adding to her natural beauty. She was a gorgeous sister, with incredibly smooth skin, who never wore any type of makeup. She was also an extremely devout Christian woman, yet very cultural who most times wore long fitting colorful dresses. She turned on a lot of men. No one knew if she did it on purpose but regardless, she always carried herself in a classy and dignified way. The way a woman does.

At that very moment Peter began to understand how his unwillingness to pursue something more concrete with Cassandra was not provoked by Cassandra herself. It was him. It was a gear within him which had remained hidden inside ever since he was a small boy in the orphanage. All religious women scared him. Not because of what they stood for but because of who religious women reminded him of. They reminded him of pain and abandonment … forms of hurt unintentionally imposed upon him by his mother. He could remember his mother and how she was so sincerely devoted to the Christian church. He could remember every Sunday being fussed over before church with his clothes and hair, during church being mobbed by religious women who thought he was so adorable, and after church during the reviews with his mother to discuss what was discussed at church. Then the sudden and unaccepted departure from the only woman he had ever loved in his life. How could she leave him like that? How could God just take her away like that? He did not want to feel that pain, which still had not gone away totally, ever again. And he felt that by avoiding falling in love with a religious woman, he could avoid being hurt. Another blow so powerful could destroy him. He was falling though. With each meeting with Cassandra he began to fall even more. She had a hold on him. Whether she knew or not was unclear to him. Something had to be done. He was not willing to take any chances. Something had to be done.

"Ladies…I must compliment you on a wonderful dinner." Peter said while rubbing his stomach, "Which one of you made the cake?" Giggles came from all around the table.

"Luc is the lady who made it." Taz said as he burst out laughing, setting off a chain of laughter all around the table.

"Luc, where did you learn to make a cake like this?" Peter asked with a seriousness that caused an automatic cease of the laughter.

Luc, who was sitting quietly with his head down, looked up and answered

"I got the recipe from a magazine."

"Well! You certainly do have baker potential. This cake is excellent. Would you mind if I took a piece with me." Peter asked.

"No. I mean yeah. I mean, I don't mind." Luc said with a smile.

"Thank you. Oh...and just for the record...women love a man who can cook." Peter commented while looking directly at Taz, who was wearing an uncomfortable look. "As a matter of fact, knowing how to cook, clean, and sew adds to your manhood. It shows that you can take care of yourself. So guess what?" Peter said with a brief pause that caused everyone around the table to give him their full attention, "I'm going to be leaving town in the morning. That's what I wanted to talk to you all about. I have very important business to take care of and I'll be gone for about a month. Of course I will be calling to check on you all so don't worry. While I'm gone though, I'd like for you ladies to teach these gentlemen how to cook, and I want a meal...prepared by you gentlemen when I return." Peter continued.

"We can't teach these fools to cook." Rochelle exclaimed.

"Plus, I aint eatin nothin that those boys cook. They always scratchin and pullin on themselves. No way!" One of the other girls said.

"Okay then, fine. You all don't want to respect me anymore after all of the love I show all of you? I understand. I guess I was wrong about you all. I thought you respected and loved me as much as I do you. I guess I was wrong." Peter said as he got up to leave, in an attempt to look heartbroken.

A silence filled the room. It hung for a minute or two until Rochelle broke it.

"Okay... Okay! But Peter, you have to tell them that they have to listen to what we tell them." She said in a pouting way.

"Fellas?" Peter asked.

"Ahight." The guys responded in a totally enthused way.

"I just want you to know that this is fowl Pete." Taz said.

"Yeah man, real fowl." another boy echoed.

"Have any of you heard the saying what doesn't kill you only makes you stronger?" Peter asked.

"Yeah." The guys responded.

"Well, this is one of those instances. Taz, you should certainly understand where I'm coming from." Peter replied while looking hard at Taz. "Besides, what's so bad about learning how to take care of yourselves? Now I have to go. All of you get over here and show me some love." Peter ordered with a smile.

All of the teens got in a line, hugged Peter, and then began to clear the table. Some headed up stairs because it was not their night to clean up. As Peter bid farewell to Cassandra and started to the door she asked

"All I get is a wave? I don't get a hug like everyone else? Well excuse me!"

"Cassandra." Peter replied in an exasperated way.

"What doesn't kill you only makes you stronger. I believe that's what I heard you say. Am I right?" Cassandra asked while looking in the air as if talking to someone else.

At which time Peter walked over and gave her a big hug. It felt good too. So good he held her for much longer than he had planned to.

"You can let me go now. I'm a Christian woman mind you." Cassandra said with a smile.

It was obvious she realized she was wearing him down.

"Yeah, I almost forgot." Peter said as he walked to the door.

"I'll pray for you to have a safe trip. And don't forget what I said earlier...I meant it. Every word!" Cassandra said.

"I won't. I'll see you in a month, but I'll call in a few days." Peter said as he walked out of the door and closed it behind him. "I think I love you too." He continued to himself as he walked off the porch.

Chapter
6

Both Tyranny and Jasmine had been anticipating Peter's arrival for close to two weeks. It had been a little over two months since they had last seen him but Jasmine did occasional talk with him over the phone and discussed a variety of investment options. It was true that Peter did want to purchase stock but he was also looking to purchase six or seven acres of land with which he could build a ranch house and establish a farm, sort of like the group home in Atlanta.

Peter was fully aware of the extreme gang violence in Los Angeles and he was interested in trying to provide the same type of help for youth in Los Angeles as he had so successfully provided for youth in Atlanta. His plan had always been to move youth from their original environments and get them to designated areas where they could be "worked on" in a sense without having to deal with that which they were striving to escape. He understood how changing ones location would certainly contribute to changing one's life. Having homes in other states would mean he could move some youth entirely out of their original state instead of just moving them a few miles away. Most of the youth Peter dealt with had basically no ties anyway. Of those who did have a family, most had long been abandoned by those families, and others came from abusive households which they were not interested in going back to.

Jasmine had informed Peter of an area right outside of Santa Monica which would be an ideal place for his new group home. The ground was fertile, great for planting a garden, the weather was excellent, the people in the area were pleasant, in addition to the fact that Santa Monica was not as far as Atlanta. The distance was more of a plus for Jasmine and Tyranny. Peter was pleased with the information he had received and scheduled a meeting with Jasmine. He would fly out to L.A., ride to Santa Monica with Jasmine, and view the property. If everything was satisfactory, he would immediately begin making arrangements with contractors. The design of the group home would be identical to the one in Atlanta, which meant Peter already had blueprints, and prices for materials. Establishing a total cost for labor would also be no problem because Peter was very generous when it came to that. He felt as though you get what you pay for and his kids deserved the best.

It was nearly 3 AM when Jasmine and Tyranny met Peter at the airport. Peter always liked to fly late at night or very early in the morning because there was less congestion in the airports. Jasmine and Tyranny on the other hand were not as enthused. However, considering the fact that it was Peter with whom they were going to get, neither complained. As a matter of fact they were very upbeat. It was clearly understood that Peter's visit was primarily for business purposes, yet the women owned a beach front home on Santa Monica bay and planned to spend a little relaxation time there with Peter who, Jasmine discovered through phone conversations, was long overdue for a vacation. She and Tyranny each had fairly intimate and personal conversations with Peter during the previous months, which not only intensified their fondness of him but also brought them all closer as friends.

Peter, still left without a clue as to what Jasmine and Tyranny had planned to propose to him, and still confused about his feelings toward Cassandra, was in turn beginning to develop a more than just friendly fondness for the two women. He would never make it known though. Regardless of how giddy and *high-schoolish* he felt when the women would take turns talking with him on the phone, he knew how strong a bond they had together and he did not want to cause any confusion.

As Peter stepped from the terminal both women greeted him ardently, with wide-eyed smiles and even some stroking of his arms and hands.

"Ladies! I'm honored once again by the beauty of you both. I'd also like to apologize once again for my choice of arrival but I hope to make it up to you both with dinner later this evening." Peter said as he kissed both ladies hands then held on firmly to each, which was unusual but pleasant to both.

"Now, now Peter…there is no need for apologies or dinner. You're our guest and it's we who will show you a good time during your visit." Jasmine pointed out as she further submitted herself to Peter by allowing him a tighter and more intimate grip of her hand.

"That's right Peter. We've been anticipating your visit for weeks now and would be offended if you would not allow us the pleasure of catering to you during your stay." Tyranny added as she also submitted her hand to Peter.

"Well...what can I say? I most certainly wouldn't want to offend either of you. But promise me neither of you will make too much of a fuss." Peter humbly replied as he switched his gorgeously seductive gaze back and forth between the women.

"No fuss is too much for Mr. Peter Phontane." Tyranny said with a smile.

"Exactly. Now let's get you back to our place and settled in. We have a lot planned and we'll certainly need some rest." Jasmine said as she reached for one of Peter's carry-on bags.

"You sure do travel light Peter." Tyranny said with a strange look.

"Oh no...the rest of my things will be brought to your place later. I hope it's no inconvenience. I mean, I still can arrange to stay in a hotel if it is.. Peter replied.

"Now we already discussed this Peter. There is no inconvenience. Besides, how could we live with ourselves knowing that we allowed our dear friend to stay in a hotel when he has come so many miles." Jasmine said.

"You're staying with us and that's that. You may actually enjoy yourself while staying in a house on the Bay with not one but two beautiful ladies." Tyranny pointed out as she held on to Peter's hand with both hers.

"I'm sure I will." Peter said in a low tone with a smile; mimicking what be believed to have been the casual flirting he had gotten used to from the two women.

"You two are bad." Jasmine commented as she began leading Peter by the hand toward the exit door.

Tyranny, who was still holding on to Peter's hand with both hers, quickly got in step, and all three proceeded to Tyranny and Jasmine's limousine, which was parked outside.

For the first week of Peter's visit to L.A., everything was strictly business. This meant Jasmine got to spend much more time with him than Tyranny did. But during the evenings when they got back home, Jasmine would conveniently make herself scarce so Tyranny could get an equal amount of his time. Though her time with Peter was less social, Jasmine was thoughtful like that. She wanted him to feel equally as comfortable with the both of them. After all, how else could the women get emotionally closer to him and expect him to accept their proposal.

Everything as far as the land and putting his project in effect seemed to be coming together like a very well written script. Peter had already set up an appointment with developers and contractors with whom he had been referred by Jasmine herself. Jasmine, after conferring with Tyranny, concluded that the faster all business was taken care of, the more social vacationing time both women could spend with Peter. She had already spoken with the developers and contractors even before he arrived in L.A., ensuring the fact that the meeting would be a formal meeting discussing the cost of labor, which would probably only take a few hours. Then of course there would be the initial three or four days of monitoring, by Peter, where he could make sure things were running smoothly. That would leave approximately two weeks of vacation time left for both women, and 2 weeks of much needed quality time with Peter. Scheduling and maneuvering to secure an ample amount of play time had been a bit strenuous for Jasmine but Peter was well worth the effort. She could hardly wait to see him in a bathing suit.

"I can't believe everything went so smoothly. I figured I'd have been working this whole thirty days. I guess doing business in L.A. is a lot simpler than I thought." Peter said while sitting on the patio of the beachfront home and sipping a glass of lemonade.

"Well, I wouldn't say simple." Jasmine pointed out while shooting a smirking glance at Tyranny. "But things do tend to go smoothly when proper preparation is made. You'd be surprised of how simple a complicated situation can become when the proper preparation is imposed." Jasmine continued.

"And when the proper elements are in conjunction I might

add." Tyranny mentioned.

"I agree." Peter responded with a blank smile. "But you know what? Sometimes when we're all talking I get this faint impression that you two are talking about a little more than the subject at hand. Am I wrong?" Peter continued.

"Well..." Jasmine began.

"No you're not!" Tyranny exclaimed.

"Tyranny." Jasmine said in a sort of whining way. "Not yet...okay?"

"Okay, okay." Tyranny replied.

"Um," Peter said with a slight but uncomfortable chuckle. "Am I missing something here?"

"All in due time Peter. We'll explain everything in due time." Jasmine replied.

"I hope whatever has to be explained is nothing bad." Peter said with a serious glance at both women.

"Please...don't worry Peter, there's nothing bad about what we have to discuss with you." Tyranny explained. "I noticed how you've been admiring the Bay. We have a boat docked down there if you'd like to go for a cruise." she continued in an attempt to change the subject.

"The bay is beautiful. It seems befitting for the two of you to have a home here." Peter replied.

"You should see it on a moon lit night...it's magnificent!" Jasmine cut in.

"I'll bet." Peter responded.

"Well Peter?" Tyranny asked. "The cruise on the boat?" She continued after seeing the blank look in Peter's face.

"Oh, I..." Peter began.

"Mind you...she loves speed. She even scares me sometimes.

" Jasmine pointed out.

"Not on purpose though." Tyranny said while clutching Jasmine's hand and giving her a short apologetic look.

"I'd love to go for a cruise." Peter replied. "Oh…and for the record…I love speed as well." Peter continued with a smile, as he jumped up and headed toward the dock.

That day on the bay was a blast for Peter. He could not even remember the last time he had so much fun without the kids. He felt like a teenager, and was a bit disappointed when it had gotten late. The way the moon glistened off of the water and lit up the bay, which by then transformed into darkened waters, was much more amazing a sight than Jasmine had explained. He could sit out there forever admiring what he saw. He felt as though he was in heaven floating on the bay with these two bikini covered beauties. 'They could both be models.' He thought to himself. He could not escape the thought of what the women wanted to talk to him about though. The feeling of curiosity was eating through him like ants on a deceased animal's carcass.

Peter was not the only one flattered by the presence of beauty. Both women took turns indulging in eye fulls of this hunk of a godly man. How could a man be so profoundly splendid physically yet so humble and compassionate? Seeing him with no shirt and wearing bikini bathing trunks was so intoxicating and enticing. Both, unknown to the other, even had brief fantasies of, in a sense, gormandizing this man. In fact, neither woman passed up the opportunity to nonchalantly touch Peter either while talking or whenever the boat was being sharply turned by who ever happened to be at the helm.

Both women were surprised when Peter took the controls because neither suspected he could handle a boat as well as he did. But Peter was not new to speedboats. He had lots of experience with them. Once he finished second in a boating competition he entered on a whim while vacationing in Rio years prior. Tyranny loved the speed with which he skimmed the boat over the water. Jasmine, who was sometimes slightly fearful when Tyranny rode fast, felt not the least bit timid while Peter had the controls.

"I wonder if he handles everything so smoothly and confidently." Jasmine sneakily commented to Tyranny while Peter's gaze was pinned to the horizon.

"You are so bad." Tyranny replied as she gave Jasmine a quick peck on the lips.

It was the first time they had done so in Peter's presence. Though it was behind his back both were aware of the fact that Peter had no problem with their relationship. Nevertheless, they tried, at least for the time being, to keep their intimacy out of his view. They felt as though it may have caused a misinterpretation in the proposal they had planned to make to him. Peter was by no means totally slow. Sure, he still had not yet picked up on what Jasmine and Tyranny had in store for him but he was aware of the fact that they were still intimate with each other while he was there. He had accidentally heard them making love a few nights prior. The women had inadvertently knocked the hook off the phone in their bedroom. Peter, wanting to call home to check on his kids, picked up the phone in his room only to be surprised by the pleasurable moans of enjoyment both women were receiving from each other. The incident did not bother him. To be honest he was aroused, as would most men have been, and listened a lot longer than he should have until he came to his senses and realized how much of a violation of privacy he was committing.

Jasmine's and Tyranny's level of love for each other was exactly what kept Peter so blind to what was being contemplated. He would have never imagined such a proposal would be made to him by these women. His curiosity would be no more after one evening, a few days prior to his departure back to Atlanta, when Peter prepared a delicious stir fry over rice dish which was not only one of his favorites to eat but also one of his favorites to cook.

"And an excellent cook too?" Jasmine exclaimed after a glance at Tyranny while taking a sip of the white wine the three were having with their meal.

"Okay ladies." Peter began as he wiped his mouth with his cloth napkin, dropped it beside his plated, and sat back in his chair. "I don't mean to be rude but I'd like to know what's going on. It seems as though I'm being reviewed for something and I'd like to know what. You both seem to be scoring me. Is this about me gaining credibility to prove myself worthy of your friendship? I mean, I do understand your relationship and I have no problem with it. I consider you both dear friends and I thought you felt the same toward me. I never imagined that you women would resort to such a thing as grading me just because I happen to be a man. And honestly, I'm greatly offended by both your behavior." Peter explained tactfully.

"You're right Peter. This has gone far enough. We've been regarding you as a piece of property being appraised and we apologize." Jasmine replied.

"Yes Peter...we're sorry. But what's going on is not what you think. Our marriage does not mean that we are men haters. Though we are leery of the intentions of men, we're also just as leery of women." Tyranny explained.

"Now it's true...we have been, um, critiquing you but not for the intent of qualifying you as a friend. You are already that...regardless of anything else. You are not only a good man but a good human being as well." Jasmine admitted.

"Yes, we don't meet many of those you know?" Tyranny added.

"Well what is it that I'm being critiqued for?" Peter asked.

Tyranny and Jasmine both looked at each other with looks of slight dismay, then Tyranny began.

"Look Peter...we have a proposal to make to you but it is very difficult to explain. So if you will please refrain from interrupting, it would be a lot easier for us."

"Peter, we don't want you to misinterpret this proposal nor do we want to offend you or insult you character." Jasmine explained.

"Exactly. We both know you.re a damned good man, and damned attractive." Tyranny began then paused for Peter's smile of appreciation. "But what we'd like to propose is nothing bad. Your acceptance would in no way be a contradiction of your character." She continued.

"Do you remember the brief conversation we had during our first meeting at the Investicom annual ball? You know...the one about your wife, or should I say the type of versatile woman you'd like to marry?" Jasmine asked.

"Yes I do." Peter answered.

"Well basically...we.re proposing to you. We are willing to be that versatile wife." Jasmine blurted out nervously, realizing that the moment of truth had finally come.

Jasmine, as well as Tyranny, knew the conversation at hand could lead to the fulfillment of a long anticipated desire of both women...or it could cause them to lose a very dear friend and client. After a stunned look and a brief silence which seemed to last for an eternity, Peter spoke.

"I would ask if you two were joking but it's clear you're not. And honestly ladies, I don't know quite what to say." Peter replied in a sort of blushing way.

"Peter, it's apparent from the look on your face that you're feeling, well...uncomfortable. We don't mean to put you on the spot. As a matter of fact we don't even need an answer immediately." Tyranny explained while turning her attention to Jasmine for support.

"That's right." Jasmine said, hurrying to Tyranny's rescue, "We just wanted to present the question to you. What we're proposing is much too serious for an immediate answer because what we are proposing is an actual marriage which would include all of the obligations and responsibilities. The only difference is that you'll have two wives. You wouldn't even have to move out here."

"See, though we do want you for our husband and plan to love you as such, Jasmine and I have been together for a good while and sometimes we'd like to be together...you know alone." Tyranny explained, stopping when she saw the look of surprise on Peter's face.

"You mean to tell me that you want a husband in your lives but one who doesn't live with you? If that's the case, why not just have a man without the marriage." Peter pointed out.

"Well because we want a husband, and children...just like a normal marriage, except as we pointed out...you'll have two wives." Jasmine answered.

"So exactly what other stipulations do you two have?" Peter asked.

"None." Both women answered at the same time.

"But if that's a problem, we've both agreed that you can watch us sometimes when we make love." Tyranny continued.

"What do you…!" Peter exclaimed, then caught himself after he remembered how much he enjoyed listening.

So if watching with consent made him a pervert, which is what he initially thought the women were implying, then what did listening without make him.

"Tyranny. Jasmine." Peter began while turning to each as he said their names. "I'm very flattered by your proposal but as I said earlier…I don't know exactly what to say. Individually both you women are much more than any man could possibly dream of having, and for me to be faced with the opportunity of having you both…well, I'm speechless. As you both pointed out, this marriage would be extremely complex, and it's something I'll have to seriously consider before giving an answer. Tell me though…how exactly would we get married?" Peter asked.

"We wouldn't do it in a church or anything like that, we'd have a private ceremony amongst ourselves. There we'd exchange vows and rings." Tyranny replied.

"The key would be the fact that we're all mature enough to handle this commitment without a piece of paper binding us." Jasmine added.

There was quiet, as Jasmine and Tyranny looked back and forth from each other to a bewildered looking Peter who had focused his attention on his glass of wine … circling the rim of the glass with his finger.

"I hate to ask this question but, um…" Peter began.

"Sex?" Tyranny asked.

"Well, that is a part of marriage." Peter replied.

"You're right. Now that's where we give that which we ask of you. Sometimes you and Tyranny would be alone together...sometimes you and I. And if you'd like...which is no problem for neither Tyranny nor myself ...we can all be together at once sometimes." Jasmine explained.

"Sounds like heaven." Peter said.

"It could be. See Peter, you.re sitting here explaining how lucky you would be in this marriage but you.re forgetting how special you are as well." Tyranny pointed out.

"That's right. You are an extraordinary man, inside and out. Tyranny and I both began falling in love with you from the moment we met you." Jasmine added.

"And we.re hoping, considering how deeply we feel for you, that our proposal is something that you will chose to accept." Tyranny continued.

"You ladies have passed the baton like a professional relay team." Peter began, pausing for the slight chuckles of both women. "And I must admit that your proposal was not only maturely and clearly presented but tastefully laid out as well. You're both very classy. I'm going to be flying back out here in a few weeks to check on what will soon be our new group home. I'll have an answer for you ladies then." Peter said as he got up to clear the table.

"No Peter, we'll handle cleaning up. You did cook...remember?" Jasmine said.

"Yes. So, sweetheart." Tyranny added with a smile.

"You go ahead and get some rest. You remember you promised us you'd teach us how to fish." Jasmine added.

"And you'll definitely need a good night's rest if you want to have the energy to instruct two women on fishing." Tyranny said triggering a short laugh from everyone.

"Okay I'll see you two in the morning." Peter said as he began to walk out of the kitchen door. Then he stopped.

"What is it Peter?" Jasmine asked.

"Sweetheart." Peter said as he turned half way toward the women. "That sounds nice." He continued as he walked on.

Chapter
7

For the entire time Peter had been away, the girls at the ranch home had an almost impossible job on their hands trying to teach the guys to cook. It was not like some of the guys did not know how to cook, it was their immature understanding of manhood coupled with the taunting they assumed would arise due to their willingness to go with the program. All of the kids in the home faced most of the problems they had in life basically because of their desire to be accepted. Though the home was to serve as a turning point in their lives by eliminating old habits, immediate change could not be expected.

 Cassandra understood this, which is why she didn't push too much. There were benefits to this whole project so she allowed the kids to handle certain situations themselves. But there were occasions when she had to step in and settle a dispute, most times involving Taz.

Many people believed Taz acted out merely due to the fact that he was a menace who would end up in prison for life or die a horrible death at an early age. Taz was not a bad kid though. Most kids are not. He simply did bad things because he thought it was expected of him. Most of the black males Taz knew were either gangbangers, drug dealers, drug addicts, or policemen. And even amongst the policemen, many were as corrupt as any criminal. So his idea of who he was as a black male was one of distorted understanding. And because of this he struggled inside due to an emotional war of good and evil, which ultimately manifested itself in the form of mischievous behavior.

Some days he would be off by himself, in his own world, shooting hoops. Even passersby who spoke were ignored as if they did not even exist. Other times he would be such a hell raiser Cassandra could do nothing more than pile on an abundance of extra chores to calm him down. She understood his mood swings. The other kids on the other hand were many times offended by both Taz's.

On this particular day, Taz let frustration get the best of

him. Amongst the guys at the home Taz was basically the leader. He dictated how the other guys would act, what they would do for recreation, ect. But in regards to the cooking instructions, after much trial and error, the level of sincerity shown by the girls finally began to sink in, and the guys willingly reached a point of submission. Early that morning Taz instructed the guys to refuse to cooperate. Unfortunately for Taz, this was when the guys decided to commit mutiny.

"Man, what are y'all doin'?" Taz asked surprisingly as he walked into the kitchen. "I thought we made a pact." He continued.

None of the guys said a word. The silence was broken when Rochelle blurted out,

"These young men are tired of living in your 'never land'... Captain Hook!"

The comment triggered a chain of laughter from the rest of the girls, and muffled giggles from the guys. Cassandra, clearly recognizing the anguish in Taz's face, made an attempt to ease the tension.

"Taz." She began in a soft trusting tone."Why don't you
join the rest of the guys? They seem to be enjoying themselves."

Taz looked around, clearly noticing the guys. obvious avoidance of his angry gaze of abandonment.

"Well Taz? We have an extra apron for you." Cassandra continued with a smile while gesturing to an apron hanging on a chair.

"Man ,,, fuck that! I ain't no bitch! I ain't wearin' no motherfuckin' apron and I ain't cookin' no motherfuckin' dinner! I'm outta. here!" Taz yelled as he stormed out the front door of the ranch house.

Cassandra gave chase but Taz was as quick on his feet as he was quick tempered. By the time Cassandra and the kids reached the front door Taz was already sprinting down the road. There was no way she could catch him on foot. She considered getting in the van but what would she do when she caught up with him. She had seen him out of control before, and he was extremely unmanageable. Besides, she could not leave the other kids unsupervised to chase Taz who was now considered a runaway. The proper authorities had to be notified, and they would initiate a search. As long as the runaway had not committed any crime, they would simply be taken back to the home. Because Taz was not sent to the home as an alternative to any type of detention, staying would be his decision.

Specially trained officers usually conducted the searches. Why? In cases like these, the runaways were obviously upset. Someone trained to handle them in an appropriate manner would defuse the entire situation much quicker, which was the intent. Regardless of the troublesome of the teens had gotten into, the fact that they were teens had to be kept in mind. Most kids in group homes are victims of some form of abuse. They had to be dealt with very delicately. Simply arresting them was not a rational option.

"Ms. Adams, are you gonna go get him?" Lena asked hysterically. "You can't just let him run away! You know if he goes back in the city and The Mobsters see him they might actually kill him this time!" She continued through sobs.

Everyone knew Lena loved Taz. She and Taz were about the same age and, in secret, spoke of going to college together and later getting married. To anyone other than Lena Taz would never admit how much he loved her as well. She was very pretty, with a French Vanilla skin tone, gray eyes and long wavy blondish brown hair. But it wasn't just her appearance which attracted him to her. She had proven her loyalty to him on several occasions, specifically the time when she caught him crying his eyes out one night and never told a soul. She very affectionately held him while he cried himself to sleep. She never asked any questions, and the next day acted as if nothing ever happened. Taz knew he could trust her, and to him trust was more important than anything else.

"Don't worry Lena. I'm going to call the police and pray
they get him before those Mobsters do." Cassandra stated as she picked up the phone.

"But if you do that, he'll go to Juvie." Luc exclaimed.

"No he won't go to juvenile detention. Taz is here voluntarily, so the police will..." Cassandra began to explain until the sound of a dispatcher answering the phone grabbed her attention.

After answering several questions and giving a description of Taz, Cassandra hung up the phone. Then, while leading the kids back into the kitchen to continue what they were doing, she reassured them of the fact that everything would be just fine. The Lord would not allow anything to happen to a good kid like Taz, she explained. She was a superb motivator, and it did not take long before the kids were once again preparing dinner, at which time she quietly excused herself. Concealing her own feelings of sadness, Cassandra headed to the rear of the house and into her own room where she closed the door, got down on her knees beside her bed, and began to pray

For most of the evening, the house was absent of conversation. After finishing dinner and cleaning up, the kids retreated to their respective rooms while Cassandra stayed sitting, in the dark living room, right next to the telephone. The guys all lay quietly in their beds, eyes wide opened, blaming their betrayal of Taz on the incident.

"What if The Mobsters get him." A lone voice asked in the dark.

"They ain't gonna get him. They prob'ly ain.t even looking for him no more. Anyway, just shut up and go to sleep.When you wake up, Taz will be back." Luc commented while staring at Taz's empty bed.

He knew The Mobsters were notorious. His old gang had run ins with them and he had a lot of dead homies as a result. Regardless of time...they never left a job undone. If Taz was spotted, he most certainly would be killed. But what did he do? Why does his own gang want him dead? Taz knew why, but he would never tell a soul...not even Lena, though she inquired several times. All he would say in response was,

 "You'll find out after I redeem myself with The Mobsters." That answer is what prompted Lena to automatically assume Taz was headed to the city. Though she would never betray his trust by telling anything on him, her nonchalant information about him going back to the city would hopefully save his life...and hers she felt. She would die if anything happened to him.

As Cassandra sat next to the phone, she occasionally prayed with hopes the phone would ring and someone would be giving her good news about Taz. She loved all of the kids and could not bear the thought of something bad happening to any of them. For all the years she worked for Peter only one youth had been lost. Not to death, but to the penal system. He had been given an opportunity to change his life through Peter's program but from day one of his arrival he was nothing but bad news.

His name was Aaronday Holmes and he had been released from a juvenile center to Peter. Arronday had been a participant in an armed robbery of a bowling alley that went bad and ended in the death of a bystander. He was not the shooter but was one of two to get caught. 13 years old at the time he later testified against the shooter who turned out to be the other guy who got arrested. His being released in Peter's custody was part of the exchange for his testimony. Unfortunately though, young Aaronday was much too much for even Peter's experienced staff. He constantly harassed Cassandra who, though a Christian, grew up in a very rough part of Atlanta's Westside. She was certainly not new to dealing with delinquents who made sexual advances, and handled Aaronday accordingly. She threatened him by explaining the fact that his charges for the robbery and conspiracy in the shooting were not totally nullified. One simple call to the police would be his ticket back to lock-up. He took heed to her warning, for a while at least.

Shortly after that incident, Aaronday was ultimately removed from the home by police with an additional charge of assault with intent to kill. While playing softball one day, Aaronday got upset with another youth and hit him across the head with a ball bat. The youth who was hit suffered a concussion, cracked skull, and a laceration in the back of his head which required 21 stitches. Aaronday on the other hand received an additional 10 years which meant he would be locked up with a total of 25 years. A mandatory 12 years would have to be served even before he would be considered for parole. He would spend 4 years in a juvenile corrections facility. At 17 years old he would be sent to an adult prison.

Half past 2 a.m., and there was still no call. Cassandra had been sitting in the same spot for nearly 4 1/2 hours without even
realizing it. After looking at her watch she considered calling Peter but why worry him? There was nothing he could do from

L.A. anyway. Though she did consider how upset he may be if something bad happened to Taz, and he had not been earlier informed. For some reason he felt as though he could save the world. It was inspirational Cassandra thought but she decided not to worry Peter. She could handle this.

Exhaustion mixed with worry got the best of Cassandra and she slowly nodded off to sleep. She had not been asleep very long, maybe 15 minutes, when she was aroused by a constant thumping sound. At first she thought it was her heartbeat but quickly realized the sound was coming from outside. After going to a side window and peering out, an instant smile appeared on her face. Immediately she made a phone call then went out on the front porch to finish watching Taz shoot hoops. Not knowing exactly which Taz this was, Cassandra remained silent as she walked over to the ball court. Taz never looked at her but she was sure he was aware of her presence.

"Are you o.k. baby?" Cassandra asked in a very soft and warm motherly way.

"Yup." Taz responded without looking at her.

"I know you must be hungry and tired. Why don't you come inside so I can feed you, and if you feel like it we can talk. If not, you can just go on up and get some rest." Cassandra offered in the same soft tone.

Taz responded with silence as he kept dribbling and shooting the basketball.

"Did you do anything while you were gone that I should know about?" Cassandra asked in a concerned way.

"Nope." Taz responded as he made a layup.

"Do you want me to leave you alone for awhile?" Cassandra asked. "I mean...I love you Taz, and I hate seeing you like this but if you need some space... I'll leave you be." Cassandra continued.

Tears began to fall down Taz's face and he stopped dribbling the ball in mid bounce. The ball continued to bounce to a halt.

"I'm sorry Ms. Adams." Taz said between sobs.

"It's ok, baby... it's ok." Cassandra said as she walked to Taz to hug his tall lanky frame. "Come on." She continued as she gently grabbed Taz's hand and led him into the house. This had been the first time she had ever seen Taz cry, and his uncontrolled emotion triggered a stream of tears down her own face.

Without any further words spoken, once inside the house, Cassandra warmed a plate of food in the microwave for Taz. She sat and watched him while he ate. He had a baby face and she could not help wiping the corner of his mouth with a napkin whenever he had food there. All Taz did was smile. It was one of comfort yet still uneasy. Knowing he probably did not want to face the guys in his room yet, Cassandra allowed Taz to sleep in her bed while she slept in the living room on the couch.

The next morning the kids, who all had not slept much the night before...especially Lena, came groggily down the stairs.

"Ms Adams, have you heard anything about Taz?" One kid yelled as the group stood outside of Cassandra's bedroom door.

"Ms Adams." Another called while knocking on her door.

"I'm in the kitchen!" Cassandra yelled.

As all of the kids mobbed into the kitchen, they were all caught off guard by a surprising sight, which brought smiles to all of their faces.

"Taz!" They yelled in unison.

Standing next to Cassandra, draped in an apron and holding a basket of biscuits in one hand and a pitcher of freshly squeezed orange juice in the other, Taz cooly responded with a smile,

"Ladies and gentlemen, breakfast is almost served."

Chapter
8

Peter had still not gotten over the initial shock of the proposal made him by Jasmine and Tyranny. He felt flattered yet confused about what exactly he should do. Questions of morality weighed heavily on his mind. Though he was not a religious man he wondered if accepting such a proposal would affect his credibility with the communities in which he had homes and centers. He also wondered if his staff as well as community volunteers would still respect him as much as they did at the present time. How would his kids react? Would the progress he had made with striving to get the kids to do the right thing be stagnated due to the fact they may begin to regard him as being a hypocrite?

For years Peter had sacrificed his own personal life for his kids. Though he did find purpose in what he did, and much satisfaction, when did he plan to show some love to himself? From the time he had become acquainted with Tyranny and Jasmine he had always admired them and admittedly been discreetly attracted to both. Both women had qualities about themselves which Peter was truly fond. Questions dealing with morality slowly faded from Peter's mind because after all ... standards of morality are based on religion? This was basically a divine form of dictatorship which Peter never agreed. He believed people should not try to please others especially if pleasing others caused neglect to one's self. He felt as though people should live according to their own standards as long as those standards did not affect the lives of others in a negative aspect. So why was he contradicting his own belief when dealing with his own self? He had always accepted Jasmine and Tyranny for their humanity. He saw how happy they were together, and also how non- judgmentally they dealt with others. So how could true happiness be wrong? And why did he have so many questions now?

Many questions bounced around in Peter's head as he lay reclined with eyes closed, while at the same time loosening his tie. He had always been inclined to wearing business suits on flights considering the uncertainty of who he may have met going state to state. To him, maintaining a proper business appearance was just as important as maintaining a proper business mind. Though at present, his thoughts were for separated from business. His own destiny was being contemplated. Deep inside he felt good about how the relationship...the marriage between himself, Tyranny and Jasmine could be, yet he had most times been wise enough to refrain from acting immediately off emotion. Such a move, in his opinion, was dangerous. Hasty decisions without rational analysis usually created detrimental situations, some even fatal, just as with the many youth who had died in gang or other type violence.

As Peter lay back in his seat, his sport coat, which he had taken off and hung on a designated hook above his head, fell to the floor as the plane experienced brief turbulence. Unbeknownst to him, a young light complexioned stewardess quietly picked up the coat and attempted to hang it without disturbing him. But as she went to hang the coat, the plane experienced more turbulence causing her to slightly lose her balance. Instinctively she reached for something to grab ... which turned out to be Peter's shoulder.

"Pardon me sir. Your coat fell and I was attempting to hang it but lost my balance. I'm sorry for disturbing you while you were napping." The stewardess said in a very apologetic way.

"No apology is needed. If I wasn't so careless with my coat you wouldn't have had to pick it up for me. Besides, I wasn't napping anyway, I was in deep thought." Peter replied, in his normal gentlemanly way.

"Well it just so happens I'm a college student majoring in psychology. I have a break in awhile, if you'd like to talk. It would be good practice for me." the stewardess responded enthusiastically.

After a slight chuckle, Peter responded,

"I don't think my problem is serious enough for a psychiatrist. I do appreciate your offer though. You're very considerate."

"Well if there's nothing else I can do for you, I'll be on my way. If you change your mind give me a yell, my name is Cheryl." The stewardess said as she offered her hand to Peter.

"Thank you, I will. And my name is Peter." He said as he shook Cheryl's hand.

"I know." Cheryl said as she walked away, looking back over her shoulder at Peter, and smiling a slightly seductive smile.

„Hmmm...gorgeous.. Peter thought to himself. "And nice legs too."

As Peter exited the plane and looked around, he remembered he had forgotten to call and inform anyone of his arrival, which obviously meant no one would be there to pick him up. Not a problem though, he'd simply catch a cab, which he sometimes enjoyed riding anyway because it gave him an opportunity to ride through the ghettos without being recognized.

Many youth with whom Peter had been trying to get into his programs would hide or walk another direction when he was riding through in his own vehicle. They knew he would stop to talk with them. Peter was straight forward yet tactful, and many of those with whom he spoke were slightly moved but not to the point of wanting to walk away from the lives they may have been living. There were rules in the streets. There was obligation...a loyalty to the streets. Allowing Peter to persuade them to abandon those streets would be like allowing him to cause them to neglect their obligations, which was a violation of street rules. Peter never let up though. He knew nothing good ever came without a struggle...99.9% of the time. He was deeply saddened by what he saw in those cold blooded streets but his sadness was a motivating tool which contributed to maintaining his loyalty to his kids.

"I still don't understand why you like ridin' through these slums Mr. Phontane. Nothin' but garbage! Walking garbage looking for victims to rob or kill. Seeing this everyday makes me sick. I avoid driving through these slums as much as possible. I remember back a few years ago, some hoodlums dragged me out of this cab, beat me up, and took my money bag. If I had my way I'd build barbed wire fences around all of these slums, and put armed guards in designated areas to keep all of these hoodlums in. I'd order the guards to shoot anyone who tried to get out. Hopefully they'd all just die off. The world would be a much better place." The cab driver explained.

"Maybe that's the problem, people just sitting around and complaining about the madness taking place within our communities. They don't like the gangs, drugs, or violence yet the only solution they can come up with is locking every one of us up or killing us all off. Don't you realize most of the problems in our communities stem from that exact desire? There are invisible fences around these neighborhoods preventing anyone from getting out. And the armed guards you spoke of are the oppressed themselves. Anyone who may be making his way out is usually killed or stagnated in another way. And soon, if things continue to be the way they are now, your dream of all of us dying off will come true. It's surprising to hear a black man talk so negatively about his own people. Don't you understand your lack of interest is primarily the cause of this drama? If you're so dissatisfied with our present condition, why don't do something about it?" Peter replied.

The cab was suddenly flooded with silence due to Peter putting the driver on the spot, which was his intention. He knew this professional complainer had no answer. He also know that the cab driver did not do anything to help change the problem because such an act took more effort than this close minded man was willing to initiate. It's easy to complain but for a person to initiate any type of contribution to changing the condition of his people, he must first change himself...which is also a difficult task for many.

The silence in the cab gave Peter a few moments to think of what may be running through the cab drivers mind. The pain of reality runs deep so Peter mercifully gave him a break. The driver would still remember the question even after Peter had gotten out of the cab, so Peter changed the subject.

"You know, I just got back from L.A." Peter volunteered.

"Oh yeah? I've never been that way myself. As a matter of fact, the only time I've ever traveled outside of Atlanta was the time I went to my father's funeral in Macon. How is L.A.?" The cab driver replied.

"It's beautiful! I was staying on the Bay...Santa Monica Bay." Peter answered.

"Ah, never heard of it. But it sounds nice." The cab driver replied.

"Oh...it's more than nice. I was the guest of two women who want to marry me." Peter explained, in hopes of receiving some advice though he knew this man was not actually the type of person whose advice would be valuable. Sometimes it is good to just hear what others have to say about a situation though.

"Really? Well did you choose one?" The cab driver asked.

"Choose one? I didn't have to choose one. They both want to marry me." Peter explained while staring intently at the driver's expression in the rear view mirror.

The cab driver burst out in laughter while smacking the steering wheel to add effect. "Well....if that's not jet lag talking, and two women do actually want to marry you, you better go for it. That is...if they're pretty." he continued.

"Why is that?" Peter asked

"Why is that? Do you realize how many men would kill to have two pretty women, who both know about it? Two ugly women would be twice the misery. With two pretty women, think of the sex." The cab driver said.

"Yeah, the sex." Peter responded blandly as he gazed out of the window.

It was apparent Peter no longer wanted to talk. It was appalling to think of how men, rather males, place such emphasis on sex. Though he realized his sex life while married to two women would be great, sex was not the issue. The sanctity of marriage had been totally taken for granted. Commitment and loyalty, along with the many other aspects of love have been replaced with how good ones mate is in bed, how good looking they are or how much money they have. In regards to the sex, people fail to understand the simple fact that the level of love one person has for another is what dictates how special and enjoyable sex would be. Sex is, in essence, a physical and emotional expression of one's love for another not just post marital recreation. The deeper ones love is... the better their sexual performance. Each partner will be more interested in pleasing than being pleased.

This was basically Peter's dilemma. Did he actually love Jasmine and Tyranny? Did they actually love him? It was not how much sex he could have. Though he was a modest and humble man, Peter was not so modest or humble as to not realize his effect on women. If sex was his only concern, he could probably have sex with a different woman every night. Having two bisexual wives was not really a concern either because he was open-minded enough to accept the reality of the existence of gay or bisexual men and women. What about Cassandra?

It was surprising, when considering Peter's economic status, that he lived inside the city limits of Atlanta. Most people on his financial level lived in the suburbs. Not Peter though. He lived on a normal street with normal neighbors whom he had lots of contact. Lots of money was not a motive to run away from others who happened to have less than he did. He neither considered himself better than anyone nor did he carry himself in such a way. A yuppie or snooty character would totally contradict his intentions. He did possess fairly luxurious things but his beautiful home, his two vehicles, or his expensive wardrobe did not make him. He identified with his inner self, and this was solely what his character was based on.

As the cab slowly drifted up the street, some children who were playing outside immediately recognized who was in the backseat. These children, just as many adults, adored Peter. As soon as the cab driver pulled into the driveway, even before Peter could get out, the cab was surrounded by a multitude of smiling and laughing little children. Front toothless, candied lipped, smiling little children who were ecstatic to see their hero.

"Peter! Peter! We missed you Peter!"

Greetings such as this were rewards which money certainly could not buy. Peter cherished such greetings, never taking them for granted. If he closed his eyes he could pick out distinctly each and every one of the children's voices. After all, these were not just his neighbors. With all of the various sizes and shapes, diversity, and variations of voice, Peter understood these children were him. He always believed that each race of people was a unit. And though he never treated any member of another unit inhumanely, his own unit was in more desperate need of men like himself than any others.

"Hey! How are you all?" Peter asked as one of the children opened his door for him.

"Fine!" They all yelled happily.

"Do you want us to help you with your bags?" One little girl asked.

"I don't have many. Most of my things will be delivered here later." Peter answered.

"What about those?" The little girl responded while pointing to the backseat where two carry-on bags rested.

"Well, they may be a bit heavy for you." Peter responded with a smile.

"No, they're not too heavy. I'm strong for a girl, see?" The little girl replied while at the same time sliding up the sleeve of her short sleeved t-shirt and raising her arm to make a muscle.

"Wow! I see. Okay then, you take this one and I'll take this one." Peter said as he gave the little girl the smaller and much lighter bag.

"Can I carry one Peter? I'm strong too." One of the boys asked, as he mimicked the muscle making action of the little girl yet adding a mean face for effect.

"Whoa! That's a big muscle too but I don't have any more. You can do something else for me though." Peter began as he pulled a $50 bill from his wallet. "You can pay the driver for me," He continued.

"Okay!" The boy answered excitedly.

"Are you good with math?" Peter asked with a raised eyebrow.

"Yes."

"Well, if I owe the driver $42.75," Peter began as he glanced inside the cab at the meter, "how much change should I get from this?" He continued as he revealed the bill to the boy.

The boy was quiet for a minute, with his eyes aimed toward the ground. His lips were moving but there was no sound coming out. Apparently he was doing the problem in his head. Then with a burst of life he looked up at Peter and yelled,

"He has to give me back seven dollars and twenty-five cents! Right?"

"Excellent! And for perfect subtraction... the change is yours.

"Thanks!"

"Make sure to put it in your piggy bank...ok?"

"I will. Thanks Peter." The boy replied as he took the bill from Peter's hand and headed to the driver's side of the cab.

Peter chatted with the kids for a while longer but began to feel a need to relax so he excused himself and went inside his home. There he called his main center downtown to explain how he would be visiting the homes the following day. Immediately after hanging up the phone, he called Cassandra to inform her of his arrival. He asked her to remind the guys he still expected his home cooked meal.

"Oh...they'll be ready Peter. You can bet on that." Cassandra pointed out. "But how are you? Really. You sound beat. Did everything go well?" She continued.

"Yes, everything's fine but I am exhausted. I'll explain everything to you in more detail when I get there tomorrow. Right now I need some rest."

"I understand. I'll see you tomorrow then." Cassandra replied.

Even with the marriage proposal heavy on his mind, Peter had no problem getting to sleep. He was very tired from his trip and getting to his bed was something he had been anticipating since the previous day. Calling Jasmine and Tyranny, whom he had promised to call upon his arrival to Atlanta, briefly slipped his mind. As he began to slowly slip into a much desired state of unconsciousness, a fading thought of the women reminded him of the call. And though he did not like breaking promises, he was too relaxed to get up. He decided to call them the next morning. Surely they would understand.

The next morning, Peter woke up feeling brand new. It was

surprising how just a few hours of sleep could leave him feeling so refreshed. The good night's sleep also gave Peter a clearer head with which he could rationally analyze the proposal. He had reached a point where he no longer worried about what everyone else thought. In life sometimes you are damned if you do and damned if you don't. Besides, his character would not change. It was not like he had planned to teach or try to persuade any of his kids to engage in such a relationship. As a matter of fact, Peter was not interested, in any way, in becoming an advocate for three party marriages. The marriage would be their personal business. That was it. Peter would have to accept the actuality that all human beings deserve to have a personal life. It is not selfishness. It is balance. It is healthy. Devoting an equal amount of time to one's self as one devoted to others, was in fact normal. Peter would also admit the fear he had regarding his ability to remain loyal to one single woman due to his desire to have a versatile woman. He was an extremely unique man who had met multitudes of women yet could never find one particularly special type of woman. Optimism and courtesy prevented him from believing there were none unfortunately he had never met one who produced a desire in him to commit.

With Tyranny and Jasmine ... two extraordinary women, Peter saw many positives in marriage. And though he continued to weigh his options, for the most part he had already made up his mind. However, there were still a few weeks before the women expected an answer, so he refrained from mentioning anything to either woman when he spoke to them that morning.

Peter had not planned on visiting the ranch house until later but decided to drop in about an hour early. Though he knew Cassandra would make sure the guys prepared the entire meal, seeing them in action himself would be a treat. His presence was also sure to encourage their level of confidence while at the same time further destroying the myth which says cooking or cleaning are unmanly.

Upon his arrival, Peter received basically the same type of greeting he had gotten from the neighborhood children near his home. All of the kids missed him, as they usually did whenever he would be away on business.

"Did anything special happen while I was away?" Peter asked with a smile. There was a brief silence but Cassandra, knowing how perceptive Peter was, quickly spoke up.

"No ... nothing really, just the same old thing." Cassandra began while trying hard to conceal the guilt she felt for not being totally honest. "The guys did learn a whole lot about getting around in the kitchen though. And they cooked you a lovely meal. Well it's not totally finished yet because we weren't expecting you for another hour or so." Cassandra continued while looking at her watch.

"Yeah well I missed you guys so much, I decided to come early." Peter responded.

"Okay, since you're here then, come on inside and make yourself comfortable until dinner is ready." Cassandra said.

"Yeah, you can check out what we got done so far Pete." Taz said excitedly.

"How about I just wait and you all surprise me. I love surprises." Peter responded.

Peter could already smell the pleasant aroma in the air. It was making him hungry. The time was already a quarter past four, and Peter remembered he had not eaten since very early that morning. He was certainly ready for a meal, regardless of how it tasted. He did not really lack confidence in the girls' ability to teach the boys to cook, nor did he doubt the guys' ability to learn. But he did realize that "First time" meals did not always turn out as great as people would have liked. So he promised himself, regardless of taste, he would eat all they gave him. It was the best way to keep their moral up concerning cooking. He did plan to offer pointers if needed though.

"Come and get it!" a voice sounded from the kitchen.

"I'm coming!" Peter yelled back while quickly rising to his feet.

Walking through the door, Peter was impressed by what he saw. There were homemade mashed potatoes and gravy, freshly baked rolls, steamed cabbage, and rump roast seasoned with onions, bell peppers, a dash of salt & pepper, and small potato and carrot chunks. There was also a pitcher of freshly squeezed lemonade, and three apple pies.

"Well! I must say you young men have done a fine job. I'm very proud of you young ladies for your effort to teach these young men, and young men for your effort to learn. I'm hoping you learned more than just how to teach or be taught instructions on cooking. This whole project was about unity, compromise, and gaining an understanding of manhood and womanhood. Bringing home the bacon is not always the man's job, and cooking it is not always the woman's. The main point is order. I'm not even going to ask if everything went smoothly throughout this project because I know they didn't. That's how life goes. Things don't always go smoothly but with determination you can overcome. Unity will make a lot of your struggles to overcome much easier, and a willingness to compromise will do the same. Now I don't want to talk too long because I don't want this food to get cold. I'll conclude by admitting this project was not for me it was for you, so give yourselves a hand." Peter explained, setting off a roar of clapping and whistling. "Now let's dig in." He continued as he began to reach for the potatoes but stopped as he felt Cassandra staring at him. "But first let's say grace."

After dinner, Peter sat down for a long night of conversation with Cassandra and the kids. They were all very interested in hearing about his trip and the business which kept him away for so long. They sometimes believed Peter would use business as an excuse for just wanting to get away from them for awhile. They were all so used to being looked upon as burdens and accepted the assumption that even people who tolerated them could only do so for so long before needing a break. That assumption is why they were so puzzled by Cassandra. How could someone so young and beautiful not mind being around them so much? She rarely ever took a vacation. Even when she did it was only for a day or two, usually to participate in some church function or visit the family whom she talked to frequently over the phone. But Cassandra, just like Peter was sincerely devoted to their cause. They both had their own reasons for taking on the obligation. For Peter, not only was his own upbringing a driving force but he also loved kids. Cassandra, who loved kids as well, regarded her job as a calling from God and gave her all to fulfill the calling. Neither Peter nor Cassandra felt burdened, and neither would trade their lives with these kids for the world.

Later that evening, after the kids had gone to bed, Cassandra and Peter talked more about the happenings in L.A.. Cassandra basically wanted to know if the new center in L.A. would require

Peter to be away for periods of time similar to his recent trip. She could never get enough of seeing him, and was discouraged by the fact that she may now see him even less.

"So you're going to be spending more time away?" Cassandra asked in a point blank way.

"Not exactly. I mean, of course I'll be spending an ample amount of time there during the beginning phases of operation but once things get rolling properly, my visits will be limited to about 8 or 9 one week visits per year. Now I know you're probably thinking those 8 or 9 weeks are weeks I don't actually have but I will. I'm going to limit my amount of stock investments and focus more time on my kids." Peter explained.

"Limit your investments? Well, I guess that would be a good thing. Dealing with all of that money does cause a lot of unnecessary stress." Cassandra pointed out.

"You're exactly right. I've made lots of money already and my purpose for doing so has now manifested itself. My stock playing had basically become a hobby more or less. But now I've decided to use that energy toward further building on my original cause... saving my kids." Peter further explained.

"So...have you already hired a supervisor for the new center?" Cassandra asked in a conspicuous way.

"As a matter of fact I haven't. But I'm considering offering the job to one of my present employees at one of the downtown centers." Peter responded. "Why do you ask? Are you interested?" Peter asked with a raised eyebrow.

"Of course I'm not. Why would I want to leave this house. I was just interested in knowing who you were going to hire." Cassandra responded without looking at Peter.

"And whether they'd be male or female." Peter accused with a smile while moving his head in a way to catch Cassandra's eyes.

"Peter! Don't be ridiculous! I merely wanted to know if you'd be hiring an experienced person." Cassandra responded surprised.

"And that's the only reason why?" Peter asked while waving a bible he retrieved from the end table.

Cassandra looked at Peter holding the bible in a very surprised way. Her mouth was wide opened but no words came out. Then in an exasperated way, Cassandra answered,

"Why do you do me that way Peter? You know how I feel about you, yet you've explained how you're not ready. I respect that. I try to refrain from making any advances toward you by not mentioning my feelings but then you do things to bring that subject to light … like you're doing right now by exposing my jealousy. Yes...I am jealous! No...I don't want any other woman having more time with you than I do! You know these things but because I don't want to put pressure on you, I remain patient while you sort things out. I lo..." Cassandra began before Peter interrupted.

"Cassandra...I apologize. I was only joking but now I see how maybe I should have joked about something else. I hear everything you're saying...okay? But right now it's late and we both need to get some rest." Peter said as he stood and walked toward the door.

"Subject getting to be too much, huh?" Cassandra said sarcastically.

"Cassandra." Peter responded in a drawn out begging for mercy type way.

"I'm sorry...okay? I don't mean to push." Cassandra said as she walked passed Peter to open the door for him.

"Will you be back tomorrow?"

"Yes, I won't be going back to L.A. for about 2 weeks. This trip won't be as long though. Hopefully the home will be complete soon so we can begin to move some kids in." Peter explained.

"Well, I guess I'll see you tomorrow." Cassandra said with a half smile.

"Yes, tomorrow." Peter said while walking out the door.

For the next two weeks, Peter had rarely even thought about how he would answer the proposal. Though he already knew what his answer would be, he wanted to do something more than just answer with a yes or no. Cassandra had not made his decision any easier but Peter knew what he wanted to do, and the sooner the better. He was actually beginning to feel himself becoming weak to Cassandra.

The day before his expected departure, Peter contacted Jasmine and Tyranny to inform them of his flight time. He explained how there may be a slight delay due to rain in Atlanta, so he asked them not to meet him at the airport. He did not want them left waiting without knowing for how long. Both women agreed because actually, not having to go to the airport would give them additional time to prepare for Peter's arrival. There was also one more thing Peter had to do before he left Atlanta. He had to get some things to go with his answer.

Chapter 9

The bus ride was just as saddening as it had been the previous times Margaret made the trip. Though hope always had her spirits high when she went to see Detective Archibald, Margaret was always so surprised by the negative attitudes and lack of courtesy that most of the people riding the bus had. They very rarely spoke to one another or even smiled. They'd bump by each other without even excusing themselves. An elderly person would have to stand, if there were no seats available, because no one would offer a seat. On the street downtown, people would literally walk over the homeless as if they did not even exist. Sometimes these homeless people would be yelled at or even beaten up for asking for spare change. Margaret had seen all of it before yet it was still hard for her to accept the drastic changes which had come about since she was a younger adult. In her eyes, the South was becoming just as bad as the North. Though she had never been any further north than North Carolina, she had heard stories of how brutally cold blooded the people were. She closed her eyes and slowly shook her head sadly. She prayed for hers, and hoped they had not allowed this unspeakable behavior to overwhelm them, or extinguish that which she tried so desperately, in such a short time, to instill.

Margaret's thoughts were suddenly distracted by the pressure released sound of a soda can being opened. She looked up. Her eyes were greeted by the pleasant sight of a little smiling black boy whose hands seemed too small to hold the can of soda he was sipping from. Actually, the boy was more or less sucking the soda through the small opening atop the can. Considering his size he was most likely not quite strong enough to open it completely, so he opened it just enough to get a drink. The boy stared directly at Margaret as if he could read her mind. With each of her pleasant thoughts, the boy smiled. He even offered her the can once but with a slight smile and a silent lip delivered "No thank you", Margaret declined the offer of the boy who by then had brown soda dripping down his chin. Margaret retrieved a napkin from her purse but when she looked back up to hand the boy the napkin...he was gone! A deep emotional burning began to fill her chest, which triggered the release of one single tear that ran slowly, like molasses, down her face. Why must he haunt her so? „It was not my fault!. She mentally screamed to herself. While reaching to wipe away the tear she nonchalantly glanced around to see if anyone was watching, only to be reminded of how uncaring people of the world had become. No one could feel her pain, even if they wanted to, so she left the tear alone.

Continuing to stare dreamily out of the window, Margaret noticed the big brown precinct slowly coming up on the right. This was her stop. As she gathered herself and quickly made her way to the front of the bus, she kept telling herself this trip would not be like the last. Instead of discouragement, the news would be much more pleasing. She could not bear much more of that. For approximately 30 years she had been searching only to come up empty. Maybe, as she told herself many times before, this time would be different.

Detective Cecil Archibald was an older black man, maybe 5 or 6 years older than Margaret, who had been working on and off with Margaret for a little over 20 years...without ever having charged her a dime. After hearing her extremely unfortunate story so many years prior, he had been determined to help her. But as the years went on, with frustration and the addition of other cases, his efforts became less enthusiastic. However, he had promised Margaret he would never give up as long as she did not, and he planned to keep his promise for as long as his body and mind would allow him to. He was just that type of man. Very stern, evil eyed, and a bit grouchy but compassionate. Not to mention as a detective he was one of the best in the business.

Margaret entered the precinct with an overwhelming burst of energy, expertly maneuvering her way through the maze of messy, paper stacked desks... some even customized with a handcuffed criminal. Could he, whom she had been searching for so long, have met such an unfortunate fate? "It doesn't matter" She began thinking as she made her way to the elevator. To her, as long as he was found he would still be just as precious as he had been at the time of their unfortunate separation.

After exiting the elevator, drowsy and miserable looking over worked officers half heartedly directed Margaret to Detective Archibald's office. Some of the officer's had been working in this particular precinct for years and recognized Margaret from her many previous visits. These officers were aware of Margaret's burden, and sincerely sympathized with her. On more than one occasion some even volunteered time toward Margaret's cause. They would assist by following up leads, and vowed to continue when time permitted.

It had been nearly three years since Margaret had last seen Detective Archibald, though she had spoken with him numerous times over the phone in between time. "He hasn't changed much" Margaret thought to herself as she walked into his office. His complexion was still an almost reddish light-brown tone, and he still kept his head completely bald. His bushy white eyebrows still looked as if they needed to be trimmed, and also still made a "v" shape causing him to appear angry...even when he smiled. Margaret noticed Detective Archibald still kept his face clean shaven as well, which made him look younger she thought. Even in his older years, the detective still maintained a 4 day a week ritual workout, with results that were abundantly clear. He was solid, with an erect frame similar to a professional athlete. Margaret, even with her preoccupied thoughts of her most important priority, would occasionally yet briefly dwell on how attractive a man Detective Archibald was but relations with a man, or even a social life for that matter, was unheard of at the time. There was nothing more important than her mission at hand.

"Mrs. Buckley." Detective Archibald greeted, with a deep scratchy voice and a slight smile.

"Detective Archibald." Margaret replied with a nod of the head and a smile.

"Please...have a seat. It's been a long while since I've last seen you. You're looking well...considering. Obviously you're very interested in knowing why I made such an urgent request to see you, so I'm not going to waste time with small talk. We've located some juvenile records which seem to be the exact connection we've been looking for. We have a name, though it's not the same one you gave...which was to be expected. We even have information causing us to conclude he is a resident of Atlanta. Now I know this is something we've gone through before but this time we're not doing much reaching or assuming. Most of our current information coincides almost perfectly with The information you've given us over the years." Archibald explained.

"When do you think you'll find out more?" Margaret asked.

"I have some friends in Atlanta looking into the matter right now as we speak. I also have something else to show you. Please, come around here to this computer."Archibald requested as he motioned Margaret around to his side of the desk. "Do you remember the picture you gave us?"He continued.

"Yes but surely you can't use that as identification. He was just a child in that photo." Margaret replied.

"Oh yes...we can. See, this computer is state of the art technology and it has the ability to age images. Meaning we can take this picture and age it to produce an approximate image of what the person may look like when they get older. As you can see I.ve took the liberty of doing so." Archibald explained as he pressed some buttons on the computer. "I've aged the picture you gave me and compared it to one of his mug shots. They look identical...don't they?" He continued.

"Yes they do. It looks just like him. That has to be him!" Margaret began. "Both pictures seem to be of the same person. It has to be him!" Margaret continued excitedly.

"I've been thinking the same thing. His whereabouts will be verified shortly. After that, we'll go on to step two."Archibald stated.

"And what's step two?"

"Well, step two will be to do a background check. I don't know much about this guy because I basically ran through my shots to find a match. The process was extremely tedious. I had to age, then de-age...then age again. What helped me was the approximation of age."

"When am I going to get to talk to him? I need to find out about the others." Margaret pointed out.

"In due time Mrs. Buckley. We've waited this long, so a little while longer won't hurt...okay?"

"Okay...I'll be patient." Margaret responded solemnly.

"Don't worry," Detective Archibald began while staring at the side of Margaret's face as her eyes stayed glued to the computer screen, "this is the best lead we've had yet. And I can honestly say...through all of my years of experience, leads like this result in answers." he continued.

Margaret briefly turned her head to look at Archibald in response to his statement. Then she focused her attention back on the computer screen, while staring back and forth between the pictures.

 "I'm praying. I sure am praying."

"Prayer is good."Archibald commented. My people in Atlanta should hopefully have an address for either a place of residence, a school, or maybe even a work place today. You're welcomed to remain here if you'd like. That is unless you have something other to tend to." He continued.

"No sir." Margaret said calmly. "I'm staying right here until you hear something from your people. There is nothing else more important to me." She continued.

"Okay then. How ab..." Detective Archibald began, as he was interrupted by a knock on the door."Come in!"He answered sternly.

"Sir there's a call for you on line 3." An officer said as he poked his head inside the door.

Archibald immediately picked up the phone.

"Yes." He said into the receiver.

As he listened attentively, Margaret watched his facial expressions hoping to get an idea of who was on the other end. Archibald reached for a note pad and briefly looked at Margaret to give her an affirming head nod letting her know this was the call they were waiting for. He began to write, occasionally responding "yes" to whatever it was the person on the other end was saying. Margaret was burning with curiosity and was tempted to go over to see what was being written but she refrained.
After hanging up the phone, Archibald looked Margaret square

in the eyes with an expressionless look on his face. Then, with a slight smile he said,

"Good news Mrs. Buckley. We have an address for a ranch house on the outskirts of Atlanta. How long would it take you to get some things together for the trip?"

"Detective...I'm ready when you are." Margaret responded with a smile.

Chapter
10

"What do you think about this one Tyranny?" Jasmine asked as she reached to pull Tyranny closer to her.

"Which one?" Tyranny asked as she looked through the glass counter top down onto a shelf with a multitude of very expensive diamond wedding rings for men.

"That one right there." Jasmine said while pointing through her own reflection in the glass to a beautiful 14k gold ring studded with 9 one half karat diamonds arranged in rows of 3.

"Oh Jasmine... it's gorgeous!" Tyranny exclaimed. "It almost looks just like ours." She continued.

"I know." Jasmine agreed. "That's the one we have to get." She continued as she looked up for a salesperson.

"But Jasmine we're still not totally sure of Peter's answer. Maybe we should wait until he gets here then go from there."
Tyranny pointed out.

"You heard how he sounded over the phone when we brought up the subject. If he hasn't already decided yes, then he's very close to it. And it would be wise for us to not only do what's necessary to persuade him but also be prepared for a yes." Jasmine explained.

"You do mean persuade and not manipulate...right?" Tyranny asked as she gave Jasmine a peculiar glance.

"Potato, Pototto, sweetheart...we do both want Peter for our husband right?" Jasmine responded.

"Yes but..." Tyranny began.

"But you don't want to play games with him. Well neither do I. What I do want is to secure the fact that we all end up being together. Am I wrong for that?" Jasmine confessed.

"No. No you're not. And I didn't mean to accuse you of anything. I just want us to keep everything on the up and up...okay?" Tyranny said as she reached for Jasmines hand.

"We will." Jasmine responded with a smile. "We'll nix the ring idea but let's put together a real nice dinner for Peter to sort of give him another taste of what it is that he'll be getting into." Jasmine continued.

"Agreed." Tyranny responded.

"Shall we shop then?" Jasmine asked with and outstretched hand.

"Well...I guess since we're here in this mall we may as well buy something, right?" Tyranny responded with an innocent shrug and smile.

"And they question our womanhood." Jasmine commented, setting off laughter between both women as they proceeded hand in hand on their shopping spree.

Peter had already had the pleasant opportunity of feasting on Jasmine's and Tyranny's cooking. So the honey roast duck, accompanied by candied sweet potatoes, steamed buttered rolls, and wild rice was not out of the ordinary. Though it would be delicious...not to mention, finely served both women decided to abandoned their wearing aprons idea just minutes before Peter arrived. They women wanted Peter to recognize their womanly characteristics but they felt as though the aprons may have been not only overkill but convey a stereotypical message. The very ancient "*wives and kitchen*" theme was not very popular with these ladies.

RRRRing! RRRRing! RRR...!

"Yes." Tyranny said as she answered the phone. "Ms. Elliot speaking." she continued.

"Ms. Elliot, you have a guest...a Mr. Peter Phontane?" A voice responded through the phone.

"Yes. Send him up please. Thank you."

"Yes ma'am." The voice responded again before hanging up.

"Jasmine! Peter is on his way up! How do I look?" Tyranny exclaimed excitedly.

"Gorgeous sweetheart. And me?" Jasmine responded.

"Stunning." Tyranny answered as she puckered her lips to receive a short kiss from Jasmine.

Both women made slight adjustments to their clothes and stood hand in hand in front of the opened door to wait for Peter. After what seemed to be a lifetime, Peter stepped off of the elevator resembling a male model, both women thought. Not only was he naturally beautiful but his outfit was very well put together. The off white baggie pants with matching vest; the Old English style button down silk white shirt; all combined superbly with a copper brown crocodile belt, matching shoes, topped off with a brown derby...tilted slightly to the left to add effect. He looked as though he had stepped directly off the pages of a magazine not a plane.

"Peter!" Both women exclaimed as each extended a hand to Peter.

"I thought we agreed you'd be staying here with us, regardless of what your answer would be." Jasmine said in a puzzled way.

"I hope this isn't an indication of what your answer is going to be." Tyranny followed as she looked disappointedly from Peter to Jasmine.

"First of all...how are you two vivaciously beautiful ladies doing?" Peter asked as he kissed each extended hand.

"We're fine but..." Jasmine began before Peter interrupted her.

"Great! I'm well myself. Now are you going to invite me inside or are we dining out here tonight?" Peter asked sarcastically.

"Pardon us Peter, come on in. I'm sure I also speak for Jasmine when I say the anticipation of your answer has us both very concerned. You obviously didn't come directly here from the airport considering your fresh look. So you apparently have a room booked somewhere which could only mean you don't plan to stay with us. Meaning your answer isn't going to be good and...." Tyranny rattled off hysterically before Peter stopped her with a gentle squeeze of her hand.

"Tyranny please, slow down. Yes, I did book a room but I'm not going to be staying there. I merely wanted to change and freshen up before I arrived here. My plans are to stay here." Peter explained.

"Well that's a relief." Tyranny said as she stepped closer to hug Peter.

"Yes it is." Jasmine agreed as she followed Tyranny's lead.

"Whatever you ladies have prepared to eat smells outstanding." Peter commented as he walked toward the kitchen area.

"Just a special something we prepared for the occasion." Jasmine explained. "And speaking of occasions..." She continued.

"After dinner, okay? I'm starving. And my answer comes with lots of conversation and explanation. So we'll get to it after dinner...please?" Peter jokingly pleaded.

"Okay," Tyranny answered as she once again gave a concerned look to Jasmine.

"Yes, that's fine Peter."Jasmine agreed, while expressing the same concerned look.

Peter, comprehending perfectly the discomfort he was causing Tyranny and Jasmine, though slightly amused, was not into game playing. He was not intent on making the women uncomfortable. His intent was merely to formalize the situation. Peter totally understood the serious nature of what was at hand and how delicately things would have to be handled but he did not want to dive head first into an answer as if he were deciding on which pair of shoes to wear.

During dinner, Peter made all sorts of small talk in an attempt to avoid the unspoken topic which lay as naturally in the eyes of Jasmine and Tyranny as the color itself. Both women, not totally understanding Peter's intent, misinterpreted his abundance of small talk as a tactic to sort of water down a negative answer. And due to pressure, the unspoken topic was thrown on the table by Tyranny who could no longer maintain her patience.

"I'm sorry Peter but we've waited an excruciating two weeks for an answer to our proposal, and honestly...I can't bear to wait another minute." Tyranny explained.

"I have to agree with Tyranny. Granted...we do both understand how difficult this situation has probably been for you. Honestly 2 weeks is extremely insufficient in regards to deciding to marry someone. Or some two in this case. But you did say you'd have an answer by now, so please...don't torture us any longer." Jasmine pleaded.

"You're both right. This proposal has been weighing very heavily on my mind. You have to both admit the whole idea is extremely unique however I have made a decision." Peter explained.

Silence fell over the room as Peter looked deeply into the eyes of first Jasmine then Tyranny. Both women could feel the intensity of his emotion. It was as if his soul had briefly embedded each of their souls causing each of them to smile a smile of deep emotional satisfaction, while at the same time each feeling as though they were being almost magnetically drawn to Peter. Each sat still though, mentally closing their eyes and basking in the passionate mist which Peter's eyes showered each of them.

"Ladies." Peter began as both women were simultaneously shaken out of what seemed to be a trance. "I'm sure you know how I feel for you both. Individually you're each very incredible women, and as a unit you're indescribable. The idea of me being given the opportunity of having you both as my wives is beyond

words. And quite frankly, the question of whether or not I'm prepared to handle such a complex situation has been a concern. Marriage is a lifelong journey but I trust you ladies. I believe in your ability to both be good wives as well as your willingness to help me to be a good husband. So...yes ladies, I accept your proposal. I'd be honored to be your husband and to have you both as my wives." Peter continued with a smile as he pulled two ring boxes from his pocket.

Both women were speechless, and only capable of staring at Peter as he slowly approached. They held hands in an attempt to remain calm though Tyranny's leg bounced nervously. As Peter retrieved the broom, tears began to roll uncontrollably down the faces of both women.

"Ladies...with these rings I offer my total lifelong commitment and unconditional understanding in this marriage. I love you both." Peter voiced as he laid the broom on the floor.

After placing a ring on the finger of each woman, all three held hands. In unison, as if practiced, the three jumped the broom. Peter could not help but admire how lovely an addition his rings were to the rings already present on each woman's finger. Jasmine was the first to leap into Peter's arms as he stood admiring. Without saying a word she kissed him, opened mouth and more passionately than anything Peter had ever experienced in his life. And while he still savored the softness and perfect kissing moistness of Jasmine's lips, Tyranny repeated Jasmine's welcome to the family kiss while also pressing her amazing body hard against his. He was almost dizzy, and very aroused as he had been many times before while in the presence of both women. This time was different. Both women were now his wives which meant fighting any physical indication of his arousal was not necessary. The tightening and stiffening of his male member would no longer be inappropriate he thought to himself. So he allowed the erecting process to continue. Both women were also aroused and when Tyranny felt the growth in Peter's pants, she knew it was time.

"Peter." Tyranny said calmly as she looked into his eyes. "Are you ready to consummate our marriage?" She continued as Jasmine touched Peter gently at the small of his back.

Peter smiled ever so slightly, which was a non verbal indication that he in fact was. And with no more words, both women led Peter by both hands to the bedroom. That night Peter was exposed to the most extraordinary love making imaginable. The pleasure he experienced was conceivable to only a person who had actually taken part in such an act. It was almost magical. Everything seemed to move in slow motion, as if taking place under water. Peter never knew making love could be like this. His level of endurance also came as a surprise to him but it was not his doing alone. Jasmine and Tyranny knew how to make it last, and they too were experiencing something magical. Peter's hot staff seemed to have a perfect sense of hitting the most pleasurable places inside each of their soft and slippery most sacred places. That staff also belonged to a man with whom they both loved, which heightened the erotica.

Both women experienced multiple explosive orgasms which contributed to their extreme exhaustion when they were finished making love in the early morning hours of the next day. Soft I love yous and light pecked kiss sounds faded slowly as all three fell deeper into their sleep, with Peter laying almost spread eagle in the middle and both women cuddled comfortably on both sides of him under each arm. It would not be learned until later that both women conceived that night. Conceptions which would open the door to many unanswered questions...asked and unasked by Peter, Jasmine, and Tyranny.

During the entire week Peter visited, the freshness of the marriage was apparent by the friskiness of all three. The official ceremony, which took place in the condo, included moderate decorations, candles, the reciting of personally written vows, and dinner prepared by all three newlyweds. It was very memorable to say the very least. No guests were necessary because this was all personal, and would be kept that way. "No outside interference" the three agreed. There were no plans to intentionally hide it from anyone but they also had not planned to openly disclose the existence of the marriage either. They would carry on normally and allow this very unique marriage to manifest itself to the world. Any questions would be answered honestly but not extensively, nor would any explanations be offered. This marriage involved three people. Explaining to everyone else was irrelevant.

"What about Cassandra and the kids?" Peter thought.

When knowledge of the marriage reached them, would an explanation be expected? Yes it certainly would. Peter had not a clue as to how exactly he would explain it. Would it be deceitful to intentional hide from them? Of course it would. But without intentionally hiding it, how else could it be kept discrete? The two wedding rings on his ring finger, which his wives thought of, would surely raise suspicion. Yet each wife giving Peter a ring seemed appropriate. If no one else noticed, Cassandra certainly would. Thus, the first spousal dilemma arises, and Peter thought it only best to discuss it with his wives.

"Based on what you've told us about Cassandra, she won't be too pleased about our marriage." Jasmine admitted.

"No she won't sweetheart. So if you'd like to hide the marriage from her for awhile, then I wouldn't feel disrespected." Tyranny explained.

"Neither would I. But eventually she will find out, and it will be something she'll have to accept." Jasmine pointed out.

"You're right. I just don't want to hurt her, nor do I want her to react in an irrational way, like quitting her job. She has developed a bond with the kids, and her leaving, especially over such circumstances could cause even more problems." Peter responded.

"I see your point sweetheart." Jasmine said in an understanding way.

"I suggest we do keep it hidden from Cassandra and the kids until we can all come up with a rational solution." Tyranny suggested.

"I agree. I mean after all...the problem of one is the problem of us all, right?" Jasmine asked rhetorically.

"Thank you. I'd like for you both to plan a trip to Atlanta. I think it'd be a good idea to slowly acquaint you both with Cassandra and the kids. I believe once they begin to see how wonderful you both are, acceptance won't be as difficult for them. Well...at least for everyone besides Cassandra. Considering her religious beliefs, along with her fondness of me, she'll probably never accept it." Peter explained.

"I don't think it would totally be her religious beliefs because plenty of men in the bible had more than one wife. Jacob was one of them, and he was a chosen one of God." Tyranny pointed out.

"Yes but Leah and Rachel were not engaged in a marriage before Jacob met them." Jasmine remarked in a joking way.

Chapter 11

It had been a little over a year since Taz had last seen any of the other members of his ex gang, yet for reasons beyond anyone's understanding he desired to meet with them. Though, not hard for others to see, Taz could not grasp the reality that he was not wanted by his ex gang. Believing they were in some way looking for him, he strongly desired to let them know where he was. He had plenty of opportunities to inform them but because he promised Peter he wouldn't go back just yet, Taz stayed away. Nevertheless, the desire to reunite with his so called "brothers" grew more with each passing day. He wanted them to at least know he was still alive, while also wanting to know why they had not been around when he was shot. Peter knew, which was why he forced Taz to not only promise he would wait awhile before he went back but tell someone when he decided to do so. Taz needed an explanation. There had to be some type of mistake. The voice he heard had to have been someone else!

Taz laid awake for most of the night staring at the ceiling, replaying the whole event in his head over and over again as he did many nights before. He had just left the arcade and hit the alley which would have led him straight to "The House" which was actually an abandoned crack house turned club house occupied by "The ATL Mobsters." Taz noticed rival gang members going inside a movie theater on the opposite side of the main avenue he was on just before he swiftly turned into the alley. There was no way they saw him but even if they had, none of them was fast enough to have gotten passed him and crouched for ambush. Such a person would have had to have been invisible. Who else could it have been though? Who would have known to wait there for him? Though he used the alley many times, there were other routes he had used to get to "The House." Who else would have known he would be there besides Pokey who called and ordered him to meet him at the house?

The alley was very dark as it usually was at night. Heavy drizzle had begun to fall so Taz pulled the hood on his hooded sweat shirt over his head. He also wore a ball cap, which he pulled down snug on his head because the rain began to pick up. The wind blew slightly toward him which caused the small rain drops to shower his face so he hunched over a bit and walked with his head toward the ground in hopes of avoiding the silent attack of raindrops on his eyes. All at once he was suddenly stricken with a spine tingling eerie feeling.

As he walked there was a splish splashing sound with each step. In an attempt to hear clearer in case someone tried to approach, he softened his steps. He also tightened his grip on the 32 special he had in the pouch of his sweat shirt. With the steady drizzle though, his sweat shirt slowly began to get soaked. The moisture between his palm and the pistol grip of the gun became abundant. He wanted to dry his palm but he sensed trouble, and extreme caution would not allow him to let go of the gun.

Taz approached the intersection which marked the completion of the first block of his three block journey.

Momentarily he contemplated turning off and continuing on another route but laughed to himself instead.

"All that weed I been smokin. got me p-noid." He spoke out loud following it with a slight chuckle.

Besides, turning off would probably lead him into trouble rather than away. He decided to continue on what he considered the safer route, so he walked on. As he approached the middle of the second block of his journey, the eerie feeling began to intensify. His body seemed as though it was freezing and his pace began to involuntarily slow down. Twice he looked back but saw nothing. The rain slowed to a misty breeze so Taz quickly flipped off the hood, dried his hand on the shirt he wore underneath the sweat shirt, gripped the gun again, then picked up the pace. He could see, in the distance, the end of the second block approaching but the intersection was not as brightly lit up as the first. It was a sign of being deeper into the "hood", where most of the street lights were either shot out or were so dimly lit they may as well have been out. It was unusually quiet for some time too. Then out of the silence, from behind him, a familiar voice called out

"Taz."

The familiarity of the voice seemed to ease lots of tension, so as Taz turned around he was smiling. The smile quickly turned to a frown though when he saw no one behind him.

"Ah'ight. Ya'll niggas stop bullshittin." He responded with a nervous chuckle.

There was no response.

"Yo man. What the fuck's up?" Taz asked in a worried way.

Out of his peripheral vision Taz saw a figure approaching. Instinctively he began to pull out his pistol but he was not quite fast enough. In what seemed to be a split second, he heard a voice yell,

"You fucked up nigga!"

At that exact moment, Taz was stricken with a force which resembled a swinging sledge hammer, followed by a burning which he had never before experienced in his life! He had been shot! He was knocked off balance and dropped his gun! While not yet even in a full stagger, he was shot again...then again! The whole world seemed to be spinning out of control! Taz could not get his thoughts together because everything was happening so fast! He could not breath! And darkness, even darker than the night itself, began to engulf him. He could not regain his composure, and in an instant the ground came up and smacked him in the face so hard that he was almost knocked completely into unconsciousness.

The pitter pattering of rain droplets rhythmically hitting the pavement all around his head was the first thought which registered in Taz's mind as he began to regain his perception of reality. The world had briefly gone ahead of him but he was now beginning to catch up. The situation at hand was now manifesting itself slowly. The salty taste of blood mixed with water filled his mouth as he lay face down on the cold wet pavement. There was an extreme burning, though more intense in his chest and stomach, all over his body as if it was on fire. He wanted to move but his limbs did not immediately respond.

"Somebody help me...I'm shot." Taz mumbled.

He attempted to yell but only had the strength to conjure a whining whisper. He began to cry, slowly accepting death as it crept upon him like a spider mounting a fly to consume it.

Unable to move, he just laid there crying, while making more useless attempts to yell for help. Suddenly, his legs as if with a mind of their own, began to move. His arms, following the lead, also began to move. His will to survive was motivating his body to crawl. His own inner strength, which seemed to be beyond himself, was striving to save his severely wounded body! He crawled toward the light, not realizing the light was in the opposite direction of where he initially intended to go but he kept crawling. Occasionally he made attempts to stand but the pain was too much, and he couldn't.

As Taz made it to within about 20 yards of the intersection, he could hear the fading voices of people who seemed to be about his age. He could not make out any words though because he was still too far away. He began to feel himself losing consciousness and tried to fight it but unconsciousness engulfed him, and Taz drifted off into a deep sleep. Fortunately for him, crawling had helped him escape the claws of death. A group of teens headed for a late evening function at one of Peter's centers in the city, spotted Taz as they crossed the intersection of the alley. One went for help while the others stood watching Taz. After Peter had been alerted he jumped in one of the centers vans, and Taz was immediately rushed to the hospital where he miraculously recovered. He had been shot twice in the chest, one bullet puncturing his right lung, and once in the stomach. He was very lucky to be alive, and even luckier to have been acquainted with Peter.

Taz tried hard to forget about gangs, and focus on prioritizing his life as Peter frequently stressed but there was still that void. There were also too many unanswered questions. Taz felt as though he could not move on without knowing why and by whom he had been shot? And where were his brothers? Surely the gun shots should have alerted someone. There was also the very familiar voice. Could it have actually been one of his own, sent to do him in? Why? He had not done anything wrong! It had to be a rival gang.

„Shit.. He thought. „My brothers probably already got some revenge for me. Yeah, that's it! And they ain't tryin' to find out where I'm at because they think I'm dead..

There...that was his explanation. It was the one he used to help satisfy his desire to have answers. But it wasn't completely concrete. Deep inside he knew his theory was about as solid as Swiss cheese!

Still early on a Wednesday morning, it was the guys' day to make breakfast. After the wonderful meal they had prepared for Peter weeks before it was decided by Peter and Cassandra that preparing meals would be a chore now split between the guys and the girls. The guys did not mind much because just as with almost all that males do, they turned the newly designated responsibility into a competition. They would always attempt to out do the girls. On some occasions Cassandra, who was enjoying the great meals prepared by both the guys and the girls, would secretly admit the guys had succeeded in their mission. Taz, usually excited on the guys cooking days, was moping around as he had been for the previous few days. This conveyed non verbal instructions to leave him alone. He would perform his duties as far as contributing to the cooking but that was it. Any other conversation was nonexistent. Cassandra, though slightly intimidated by Taz, always did what was necessary to maintain her respect. She never showed any weakness when Taz was in his mood. Regardless of anything else, she was still in charge. Not to mention she was an adult. Taz respected that. The other kids in the group though, were very fearful of Taz when he was in a bad mood. He was extremely unpredictable, in addition to the fact that he was affiliated with one of the most notorious gangs in the city. Sure he was young and silly at times but due to many years in the streets he was potentially violent. Taz knew of the fear he instilled in the other kids, and would many times take advantage of the fact to and extent. Truth be told, he would never do anything to harm any of them. He loved them. They were his friends and his family.

When breakfast was prepared and set on the table, the girls were called to the kitchen. After everyone was seated, Cassandra asked Taz if he would like to lead in grace. Knowing it was more a request than a question, Taz agreed.

"Our father, Lord in heaven..." Taz began as Cassandra watched him closely in hopes to recognize any change in mood.

Being such a firm believer in Christianity, Cassandra felt as though prayer could conquer all. Once Taz finished with "Amen", followed by the amen's of the other kids, he looked over at

Cassandra and gave her a slight smile. Cassandra, interpreting the smile to be a sort of "thank you...I needed that" type gesture, asked

"Are you feeling better?"

"Yes ma'am, much better." Taz responded with an even bigger smile.

It was not necessarily the prayer itself which lifted weight off of Taz's heart and mind, it was the whole scene. It was the admiration and love which Cassandra and the others had for him.
It was also the unity...without condition. He did not have to shoot anyone or rob anyone to receive their love. This love was genuine, unlike the so called love from his "brothers." Everything was different. Though he wanted to make himself believe that gang affiliation is what he wanted...it wasn't. But it was all he felt he deserved. That is until he came to the group home and experienced real love!

Chapter 12

"Good morning sweetheart. How are you feeling?" Tyranny asked Jasmine as she stood near the kitchen counter preparing cups of coffee for the both of them.

"Well...it's not as bad as yesterday but..." Jasmine responded as she entered the kitchen slowly while holding her stomach. "You're rather perky." She continued.

"I wouldn't say perky exactly but I'm feeling better." Tyranny explained as she joined Jasmine at the table with both cups of coffee in hand.

"Umm, thank you sweetheart." Jasmine said as she took one of the cups from Tyranny's hand and immediately took a sip.

"I made appointments for us to see Madeline later this morning. Hopefully we can get diagnosed and a prescription all in one wop." Tyranny mentioned as she took a sip of coffee.

"That would great. I just can't understand how we could both be so sick. It had to be something we ate. Did Peter mention anything to you about being ill before he left yesterday?" Jasmine asked.

"No. But you know how men are. They won't say anything immediately but then..." Tyranny began with a smile.

"Yes...big ole' babies." Jasmine responded with a chuckle.

"I think we should call him later after we see the doctor." Tyranny suggested.

"That's a good idea. It would also give us a chance to just talk with him. I sort of miss him already." Jasmine responded as she looked dreamily at Tyranny.

"Me too. But we'll have to get used to his occasional absence." Tyranny pointed.

"You're right. He's just so..." Jasmine began as she searched Tyranny's eyes for a description.

"Uh ... incredible?" Tyranny blurted out.

"To say the least." Jasmine responded.

"The very least." Tyranny pointed out, which set off a bit of laughter between the two.

After their coffee, which was normally the extent of their breakfast, both women showered and got dressed for their appointment with their private doctor Madeline Umbaru. Dr. Umbaru is a South African woman who had been their doctor for most of the years the two had been in L.A.. Dr. Umbaru was as much a close friend as she was a doctor to the women. They were not only on a first name basis but Madeline was fully aware of the marriage, and supported it just as much as any heterosexual marriage.

From the description of the symptoms, Madeline knew right away why both women were sick but she did additional tests to be absolutely sure. She had known about the desire of Jasmine and Tyranny to have children, and did not want to be mistaken in her findings. So after an abundance of tests, both pregnancies were confirmed.

"You ladies have been keeping a secret from me." Madeline began with a hard smile. "When I saw the rings I wasn't absolutely sure but now I know. Ladies...I am pleased to announce that you are both expecting!" Madeline continued in a very excited way.

Both Jasmine and Tyranny were ecstatic! They were speechless! All they could do was hug and cry tears of pure happiness.

"Congratulations mommy." Tyranny said as she wiped tears from Jasmine's face.

"And congratulations to you too mommy." Jasmine responded with the same tear wiping action.

"Ladies...please don't keep me in the dark any longer. I have to know about...about this!" Madeline said as she excitedly gestured her hands toward the stomachs of both women.

After explaining in joyous detail after joyous detail, both women were in a rush to call Peter and inform him of the wonderful news. He was going to be a daddy...twice! Considering his admitted desire to have children of his own, anticipating how pleasing the news would be to him was not difficult at all! He would probably want to immediately fly to L.A. to check on them but for pregnancies only days gone, an immediate trip was not necessary. It would probably be weeks...or maybe even months before they would have to begin planning for any pregnancy leave from work, which would be the time when the women would need additional assistance. They had been taking care of each other for years, and would continue to do so for the rest of the years of their lives. But with both women being pregnant at the same time, which seemed only appropriate, additional support would be needed as well as appreciated. It must also be remembered Peter was now a part of the marriage. The women would have to keep this in mind. Peter was a husband, and now father, whose character would allow him to play no part less than that of natural obligation.

The phone conversation was exactly as the women expected. Peter was just as excited as they were, and as they had anticipated he considered traveling back to L.A.

"So I'm going to be a daddy … twice!" Peter repeated for the hundredth time during the conversation.

"Yes sweetheart." Jasmine answered from one phone.

"And we're going to both be mommies." Tyranny added from another phone, setting off small joyous giggles between the three.

"Well don't worry about anything. I'll call and arrange a flight for later this evening and..." Peter began.

"We're both fine at present. We'll just wait to see you at the end of the month as we discussed." Tyranny explained.

"Yes sweetheart, we've got everything under control for now. The sickness we were both experiencing, as explained by our doctor, was basically a result of the new little life inside of us. As the babies grow, we'll experience occasional sickness but it's all natural, and we're both prepared for what's to come." Jasmine explained.

"We will in fact need emotional support and lots of pampering." Tyranny pointed out.

"Lots of pampering, huh? Well is that all I'll be needed for?" Peter asked in a searching-for-sympathy type way.

"Sweetheart..." Jasmine exclaimed in a drawn out way.

"Of course we need you for more than that! You're our husband and we love you. We are merely speaking of the pregnancy." Tyranny explained in a soothing way, after immediately realizing she had unintentionally attacked the proverbial "male ego."

"Yes sweetheart, don't misinterpret what's being discussed here. We don't want you to feel as though we're trying to exclude you. We just realize you have responsibilities there, and we don't want you flying all the way her unnecessarily." Jasmine added.

"Well, it wouldn't be totally unnecessarily. I mean I would get an opportunity to see my wives. Is that so bad?" Peter responded.

"Ohhh...that's so sweet." Jasmine said in a whine.

"Yes, sweetheart...it really is sweet. And no there is nothing bad about that. So I'll tell you what. Do you remember we discussed our visiting you in Atlanta?" Tyranny asked.

"Yes ...that's a great idea! Considering our pregnancies, it would be a good time for us to begin getting acquainted with your kids." Jasmine pointed out.

"And we'll get an opportunity to see the women who has the hots for our husband." Tyranny said.

"Tyranny!" Jasmine exclaimed.

"Wait a minute Jasmine. Tyranny's right. I mean, I wouldn't refer to Cassandra's admiration of me as being the "hots" but I do think it would be a good time to begin the, um, revealing process so to speak. Slowly but surely, I'm going to have to reveal my marriage them. I'm extremely proud of having you both, and I'd like to be open about it." Peter explained.

For the rest of Peter's day, he wore this enormous yet indescribable glow. To many, this glow was attributed to his normal positive attitude but to others, specifically Cassandra, there was something different about him. She watched attentively as Peter smiled his extra hard smile, and displayed a nobler expression on his face. It was the look of a daddy...twice. What if one of the women had twins? Would that mean Peter would be a daddy … thrice?!? Then what would it be if both women had twins? Peter giggled slightly to himself at just the thought. Was it cockiness which made him think that not only did he have the ability to impregnate two women in the same night but also impregnate them both with twins? No, it was not cockiness. The thoughts were merely thoughts...contemplation of a variety of outcomes which bathed Peter in a sea of pure elation. Two girls maybe? A boy and a girl? Two boys? Two girls and two boys? Three boys and one girl? Four girls? Peter giggled more to himself. How far apart would the babies be born? Had both women in fact gotten pregnant at the same time. During his last two visits, Peter, Tyranny & Jasmine had made love as a group twice. Peter also made love to each individually during the two nights prior to his departure from L.A.. What difference did it make? His two wives were both expecting, which pleased him to a point of absolute giddiness.

"Well! You sure do seem rather overjoyed about something today. Maybe the holy spirit has finally gotten hold of you." Cassandra said as she approached Peter who was standing on the porch of the ranch house watching the guys play basketball.

"I wouldn't say my joy stems from any holy spirit but yes, I'm feeling good today." Peter responded carefully.

"I'm glad to hear that. You still haven't mentioned those happenings in L.A.."

"Happenings? What happenings? There are no happenings." Peter responded nervously.

"Excuse me? What about the group home?" Cassandra asked with a puzzled look on her face.

"Oh! That! Yes, um, everything is going as scheduled. We're going to begin taking in kids in a few weeks. I've also decided to hire someone in L.A. rather than move someone from here."

"So I guess you've also decided not to transfer any of the kids here to L.A.?" Cassandra asked.

"That's right. I figure the kids have gotten used to the staff here, which helps in their growth. Transferring them would probably cause more problems than anything else." Peter further explained.

"Sounds good but, uh, what did you mean when you said '*oh, that*' after I mentioned the L.A. home? You said it as if you had forgotten about it." Cassandra asked in a nonchalantly interrogative way which only a woman can.

Peter was stricken with silence because he did not want to outright lie to Cassandra. Yet he could not tell her the total truth either. The seconds seemed like days. Peter was afraid of the eye contact coming from Cassandra. He thought she may be able to read him but he was also afraid to look away and blatantly admit guilt, then out of the blue came a savior...technically speaking.

"Yo, Pete, did you see that monster dunk?" Taz yelled as he ran toward the porch.

"No Taz, I missed it. Would you mind showing me again?" Peter asked as he put his hands up in a non-verbal 'pass me the ball' gesture.

"Yeah, come on." Taz said as he passed Peter the ball before trotting backward toward the court. Peter began to follow.

"Peter, we were talking." Cassandra reminded him.

"I know. I apologize but the kids need me. We'll talk later." Peter responded in a relieved way.

He would now have enough time to come up with a 'not-the-whole-truth' explanation for the question he knew Cassandra would not forget.

For the rest of the day Peter managed to avoid being alone with Cassandra but dinner had been made, served, and eaten. This meant after the girls, whose turn it was to cook, finished cleaning up all of the kids would disperse to their respective rooms. Cassandra knew this. She could clearly tell Peter was avoiding the question asked him earlier so she patiently waited until she could once again get him alone. Peter would not just rudely leave without talking to her, even if only briefly. But regardless of how brief the conversation...she was determined to get an explanation. Peter had one. Not an indebt explanation but enough to escape.

"Okay, now that you have no kids to hide behind, would you like to please answer my question? And if you don't mind, explain why you've been avoiding me." Cassandra politely asked in her usual extremely calm tone as she sat on the couch.

"Well," Peter began as he looked at Cassandra, envisioning her standing with her hands on both hips and tapping her foot." my mind had been on a lot lately due to my affairs in L.A.. You know...affairs meaning my business with the ranch house." Peter continued as he realized affairs may not have been the best choice of words.

"With the lords help...anything is possible! Cassandra said with a large smile.

Peter and Cassandra talked for a while longer about the status of all the kids. During the conversation, Peter was reminded of the "New Beginnings" annual picnic. This was a summer time event where kids who participated in any of the "New Beginnings" programs would get together for a day of games, talent shows, and lots of food. The kids were always encouraged to bring a friend who was not a member of any of Peter's programs, specifically someone affiliated with a gang or some other aspect of negative living. No gang paraphernalia was permitted on the premises though.

"Now … back to our earlier discussion. I know what you mean by affairs." Cassandra said in a sort of sarcastic way.

"Of course you do. Anyway, when you asked about my, uh, business in L.A., I was actually thinking about something else at the time, and your question was somewhat unclear." Peter explained.

"If that was all it was why have you been ducking and hiding all day as if you were keeping something from me?" Cassandra asked.

"You know you make me so nervous when you question me

about things." Peter responded

"I do? Oh Peter I apologize. I don't mean to make you nervous." Cassandra began in a really sweet voice...knowing completely well the power she possessed over Peter." It's just that I like to know what's going on with you. You're so scheduled and lonely. You keep things bottled up. I question you in an attempt to let you know how concerned I am about you, which will hopefully, in turn, cause you to open up to me." Cassandra explained further.

"And I do appreciate it. You.re a wonderful friend, and I don't ever want anything to come between us. Regardless of anything else I want you to keep in mind that our friendship means the world to me." Peter responded.

"You're emphasizing friendship obviously in an attempt to ask me to stop pushing so hard. Well I try Peter but you know...." Cassandra began to explain.

"Yes...I know. But let's just concentrate on what we already have. Agreed?" Peter asked.

"Agreed." Cassandra responded in a slightly pouting way then finished with a smile.

"Good. So how is everything around here?" Peter asked.

"Everything is fine. Taz went through another one of his occasional isolation spells but he seems to be recovering faster. The spells are also becoming less frequent. I saw you talking with him earlier. Did he mention anything to you?" Cassandra asked.

"Somewhat. He mentioned how he was still having dreams about the night he got shot and things like that but you know how he is when it comes to extensive conversation about his past. He'll be okay though. He just has some things to work out, and it's going to take him some time." Peter explained.

"I know. We give him his space when he needs it." Cassandra responded.

"Good. That's just what he needs. Hopefully, he'll soon get over it all," Peter replied.

Chapter
13

Back in Asheville exciting arrangements were also being made. Margaret had been waiting a very long time for the present happenings to occur, and the outcome could basically dictate her future. So yes, there was excitement but not the festive type. Margaret endured considerable disappointment and misery ever since her childhood in Prattville. She certainly hoped everything turned out right but caution prevented her from prematurely anticipating anything.

Though Margaret was prepared to leave for Atlanta directly from the precinct, Archibald persuaded her to go home, rest a while, and get some clothes and things together. Archibald explained how he would make arrangements for them to fly out the following week, which was three days away. After all, though he was a detective and could travel as necessary this case could be considered moonlighting. He could not just up and leave Asheville, for an unspecified amount of time, without getting permission from his superiors. And even with permission, he would most likely only have a day or two to help Margaret in her search.

Angie, while making sure Margaret got on the bus earlier that day, asked Margaret to give her a call the minute she returned home. Angie not only wanted to make sure Margaret got home safely but she also wanted to hear the news. All of Margaret's fellow employees prayed she would one day find what she had been searching for...especially Angie. She knew Margaret probably better than anyone else, which meant she was aware of Margaret's natural goodness. In Angie's eyes, Margaret did not deserve the misery she was now experiencing, and had been experiencing for so many years. God must have had a plan.

"But when Lord?" Angie occasionally begged during prayer. "When will you impose your glorious grace and lift all of the suffering from my mama's heart?" She would continue.
Though, she wished Margaret had actually been her mama, Angie only referred to her as mama during her prayers. She realized referring to Margaret as mama to her face would probably have been inappropriate considering the circumstances, so she called her Ms. Margaret instead.

Even while so caught up in her own thoughts, Margaret had not forgotten her promise to call Angie. But considering how Margaret desired rather to see Angie instead of speaking to her over the phone, she would simply catch a bus from town straight to the diner. Margaret was very fond of Angie, and regarded her as being a very dear friend. Actually, Angie was more like a daughter she never really had, and most likely would not have minded if Angie had called her mama. Margaret also decided to go to the diner as opposed to going home because it had been a few days since she had been to work. So instead of just sitting around waiting for the arrangements for the trip to be made, she would rather work to stay busy. The anticipation was already driving her crazy, and she desperately wished she could already have been on her way.

It was late evening by the time Margaret reached the diner, and to no great surprise it was packed with people when she got there. Fortunately for Angie, who was the only waitress working, the late evening crowd mostly consisted of "street people" who usually only ordered coffee or deserts. Angie's back was turned when Margaret approached the glass door through which Margaret could see her. In her own secret way, Margaret took pleasure in that fact because the surprise, with which she imagined Angie would greet her, was something Margaret absolutely enjoyed. She did not want to give Angie any time to prepare for the arrival so she actually picked up her pace, moderately and unnoticeably, in hopes of getting inside before Angie turned around.

Many people regarded Margaret as being less than normal due to her seclusion and lack of conversation but she was just as normal as any other human being, and enjoyed pleasant emotional experiences just as much as the next person. It was her burden...her miserable past and uncertain future which kept her from abundantly enjoying life. Occasionally she would indulge a bit by allowing herself to enjoy the magnificence of a bright sunny day with its clear ocean blue sky and subtle cotton-like clouds hovering above as if they were stationary. Sometimes she would enjoy the simplicity of the laughter of little children playing on the sidewalk as she passed them on her way to work. Most times no one ever even realized she was in a good mood. Well, no one besides Angie. She could sense when Margaret was feeling good and recognized her slight smile, with the corners of her mouth just slightly turned upward. Margaret's moods could also be read in her eyes. There was a barely detectable brightness. Witnessing Margaret during those rare times boosted Angie's spirit as well.

Just as Margaret had anticipated, Angie was ecstatic to see her. She literally bounced on her toes, gripped her apron with both hands, and smiled a smile so full of love that Margaret was almost immediately compelled to do the same. But it was forbidden for her to display so much joy. God was watching. Though she knew God could read her thoughts, acting on such thoughts would go way beyond the bounds of the confinement she thought God had imposed on her. In her eyes, she had done a very wicked thing. She neither had the right to be happy nor express it. The feeling was something she could rarely fight though, especially in the presence of Angie.

"Hi Ms. Margaret, how you doing?" Angie began as she rushed toward Margaret. "Come on here and sit down. I'll get you a cup of coffee." She continued without waiting for an answer from Margaret. She had gotten used to Margaret's lack of conversation. Before Angie departed to retrieve the coffee though, Margaret grabbed her hand gently, causing Angie to instantly turn around.

"I came to work." Margaret said softly as Angie seemed to be temporarily hypnotized by what she heard.

It was not specifically what Margaret said but it was the extreme humbleness in her face. It was so genuine and magnetic and warm. It was gentle and kind, and without a word conveyed the type of character Margaret possessed.

"You sure ma ... Margaret?"

Angie shuddered as she began to call Margaret mama. She had briefly been caught up in the moment. Margaret was very aware of what Angie wanted to say. And with a slightly more noticeable smile of reassurance, coupled with a few gentle strokes of Angie's hand, Margaret responded with the same soft voice.

"Yes...I'm sure."

"Well...okay. But before you start, can you tell me how things went downtown." Angie inquired.

"Everything went just fine baby...just fine." Margaret responded as she got up from the table and made her way toward the kitchen area of the diner.

Angie in turn sat for a minute basking in Margaret's strength and the word „baby.. Many older southern women referred to younger adults as „baby. but Margaret's `baby' seemed to strike Angie much more personally. It was something she cherished.

Back at the precinct Archibald, who had been making calls to his connections in Atlanta, was given some disturbing news. He was informed the trip would have to be delayed. A string of bank robberies continued to cause chaos in the city, and the detectives who were assisting Archibald belonged to a unit assigned to that case. Archibald, knowing how detrimentally effective moonlighting can be to a case, humbly accepted the fact he and Margaret would have to wait to make the trip.

"How in the world am I going to break the news to her?" Archibald began to himself while gazing out the window. "She's been waiting for a lead like this for a very long time. She'll be crushed! What else can I do? I can't lie to her. She'll just have to understand." He continued.

Before Margaret left Archibald, she informed him of how she could be reached at the diner if he needed to contact her. He should leave a message if she was not there because she would be there eventually. Archibald considered sending Margaret another telegram but obviously that would be inappropriate. So, he decided to drive by the diner and break the news.

For the entire drive he attempted to prepare a script, sort of the way he did whenever he had to inform a family of the loss of a loved one. Though, most would not regard the news he had for Margaret as being as serious as the fore mentioned, to Margaret and those who understood the situation, the news could be just as damaging. Archibald knew just how damaging because he himself was very discouraged by the news. He briefly considered going to Atlanta anyway, just to see if he and Margaret could follow up alone. The decision to do so would be unwise though, considering his connections had all of the information he needed. Besides, they had obviously suggested the delay for a reason, meaning there was no alternative but to wait.

Archibald had not immediately seen Margaret as he entered the diner but she saw him. She was uncommonly observant, and noticed any and every one in her vicinity. In her own way she had hoped perhaps one day she would recognize those whom she had lost. Upon seeing Archibald, Margaret prepared a cup of coffee and grabbed a glazed doughnut from the display case on the counter. Glazed donuts were Archibald's favorite. Margaret then hurried to greet him before he had even got in the diner good. With hands full, Margaret nudged him with her arm and gestured him toward a corner table.

"Ms. Buckley...I can't stay. I..." Archibald began before Margaret interrupted him.

"Please." She responded as she slightly raised her full hands to present Archibald with the coffee and doughnut.

Not wanting to add injury to insult by rudely denying Margaret's offer, Archibald agreed to sit and enjoy the goodies, as he normally referred to them. Besides, what officer of the law could pass on coffee and doughnuts? It went totally against the code of law enforcement, Archibald amusingly thought to himself before he remembered what he had come for.

As he sat down at a corner booth, Archibald displayed a stressed look on his face.

"Bad news?" Margaret responded, recognizing the sign.

"Well not actually bad but um ... well Ms. Buckley our trip is going to be delayed. My connections in Atlanta have been assigned to a very important case where their total attention is needed. And considering the fact that we need their assistance we're forced to wait." Archibald explained.

"Is anyone hurt?" Margaret asked while never changing her expression.

"Hurt?" Archibald responded with a confused look.

"Yes. The case your connections have. Have people been hurt?" Margaret briefly explained.

"Oh no, not directly. Actually there are a string of bank robberies taking place." Archibald responded.

"I understand. I'm not upset. I'm anxious, but I can wait." Margaret replied very calmly.

Archibald was completely thrown by how accepting Margaret was but he was pleased she was not upset. Angie, who had been nonchalantly watching what was going on, could not actually decipher the conversation due to Margaret's expressionless appearance. She wanted to move to where Margaret was sitting but she did not want to be too pushy.

"Would you like another doughnut?" Margaret asked.

"No ma'am. As I said earlier, I didn't come to stay. I appreciate this one and the coffee. It was perfect." Archibald responded as he began to stand up. "Don't worry Mrs. Buckley, we're only delayed. We will be making the trip though. We just have to be patient." He continued.

"Alright." Margaret responded as she also stood.

"I'll be in touch...okay." Archibald assured her.

"Okay." Margaret responded with a slight smile.

Angie, regarding the Detective's departure as her cue, quickly went to Margaret.

"Ms. Margaret! Is everything okay?" Angie asked in a concerned way.

"Yes baby. Everything is just fine. It will all work out very soon." Margaret responded, while still slightly smiling.

Chapter
14

The New Beginnings annual picnic was considered a momentous occasion in Atlanta due to the overall objective. Not only was the picnic a treat for the youth who participated in New Beginnings programs, it was also meant to attract troubled youth which was a method of outreach the residents of the city condoned and appreciated. Some celebrities, local as well as world renowned, donated funds while others donated time where they would either talk to youth or perform in various entertaining ways. Non celebrities also donated their services by making flyers, cooking food, or volunteering to do whatever else was needed. All contributions were valuable. The whole event was a unified effort of the people to bring about positive change, and the efforts always proved successful in more ways than one. Even if only one youth was pulled away from gang affiliations, or any other delinquent activity for that matter, the goal of the picnic was achieved.

The mood of the city was fairly up beat. Atlanta was always for the most part buoyant, living up to its informal title "Little Mecca!" There was a natural unifying quality there, with an abundance of diversity. Even with the recent criminal activity, most of the residents had enough faith in their law enforcement to remain optimistic. There was no doubt that the culprits would soon be caught, and preparations for the picnic went on without delay. Unfortunately due to the violent nature of the individuals responsible for the robberies, drastic measures would have to be taken to ensure sufficient patrol of the city. Peter would receive the news in the form of a telegram just one week before the scheduled event.

Peter:

I am sorry to inform you that due to the rash of bank robberies in our beloved city, I am forced to insist that the New Beginnings annual picnic be postponed. As governor I must admit it would not be logically acceptable to hold such an event in such a time of crisis. I pray this crisis can be expunged immediately, and normal operations may resume.

Regretfully,

Andrew

News of the postponement spread rapidly. Flyers were taken down and the mood had declined to a slight somberness which was only to be expected. The governor could feel the discouragement in the air, and was sincerely apologetic. But what else could he do. Law enforcers...detectives, F.B.I., police, ect., could not be spared. The city had to be on constant patrol, and an event such as the annual picnic would have been an extreme distraction...maybe even a diversion, which is exactly what it was going to be. Though the governor had declared the annual picnic a state holiday, most businesses and all banks were scheduled to be open for at least half the day. With this known, three of the largest banks in Atlanta were scheduled to be hit simultaneously during the morning hours of the picnic. So the news of the postponement was disappointing not only to those who were participants in the festivities, but also to the Mobsters!

"Ya heard the news?" Pokey, a member of the Mobsters, said to Ram.

Pokey was so nicknamed due to his love of stabbing his victims. Ram, which was short for Rambunctious, was the leader of the Mobsters who sat with Pokey and two other members in a candle lit room of "the house" discussing the situation.

"Yeah...I heard...so what?" Ram said with a deep southern drawl.

There was a sudden quiet. No one spoke but all were thinking the same thing. Though these were the so called officers of the gang, they all feared Ram, who was the general. Pokey, the captain, grew up with Ram and was the least likely to feel his wrath. He was usually the one to do the most talking during official meetings such as this. But he too was very mindful of what he said and how he said it. Pokey stared at Ram, thinking hard and hoping to receive some non verbal gesture which would indicate Ram's willingness to allow any question of his nonchalance regarding the news of the delay. Ram without turning his head, cut his eyes toward Pokey and said,

119

"We was gon' use that punk ass picnic as a smoke screen cause the shit woulda' been convenient. But since that bitch ass gov'nor delayed that shit...we just gon' do the shit raw dog like we been doin'. Fuck a smoke screen...ya. heard me? We ain't no mu'fuckin bustas! Anybody wanna punk out now...let me know." Ram said fiercely.

Once again it was quiet. Ram's tone was an obvious indication of his displeasure over what he considered to be unspoken insubordination. Though no one spoke, Ram was no dummy. The silence was easy to interpret. His „so what. to the news of the delay was being questioned and he despised being questioned.

"Herc...ya' nigga's ready?" Ram asked without looking up.

"No doubt." Herc answered immediately.

His name was short for Hercules due to his huge muscular build. Herc was a lieutenant and leader of one sect of the Mobsters.

"Queen Nef...ya bitches ready?" Ram asked, once again without looking up.

"No doubt."

Queen Nef, short for Queen Nefertiti was a lieutenant and leader of the female sect referred to as „The Mob-ettes..

"Everything's still set for the same time...ya. heard me?" Ram said. And without waiting for a response he continued. "y'all break!"

Herc and Queen Nef got up to leave, while making various gang signs with their hands as they exited the room. Pokey, who always stayed behind with Ram to receive additional orders, stayed put.

Ram and Pokey had been friends ever since they were very small children. Their mothers had been friends since childhood as well. Pokey's mother was killed in a drive by shooting, so Ram's mother, Celeste, took Pokey as her own. Ram's two uncles, his mother's brothers, founded the Mobsters when Ram was about 9 years old. Because of his uncles. status he moved up quickly in the ranks. He was bred to be a gangster and quickly developed his uncles' same cold blooded nature. When he was 19 years old, Ram's uncles' had been killed, along with 4 other members, in a shoot out with F.B.I. agents. Actually, they were gunned down in cold blood after they attempted to surrender themselves with hands raised. The killings were ruled justified due to the fact that two F.B.I. agents had also been gunned down in the shoot out. No one questioned the murders of the gang members due to their criminal status. Ten other gang members including Ram's mother had been arrested, charged, and sentence to life in a federal prison for various charges from murder to drug dealing to robbery. Life in a federal facility is just that...Life! Meaning neither Celeste, nor the other members arrested would ever be released from prison.

Ram, who was heir to the throne of leadership, had no problem assuming his uncles' role yet due to the fact that most of those killed or arrested were leaders, he had to rebuild. Pokey was his best friend, so it seemed only logical that he be second in command. And by beginning with mostly drug dealing and sticking up other drug dealers not affiliated with their gang, Ram and Pokey eventually brought the Mobsters back to life. It took nearly seven years but the ATL Mobsters had been reestablished as being the most notorious gang in the city. Their business had been solely drug dealing until, with the advice of his mother, Ram decided to increase the gangs money making potential through bank robberies.

"Pokey, this gon' be a helluva lick nigga. Mama said we should clear over ten million in cash alone. Ain.t no tellen' how much them bonds is gon' be worth." Ram explained, with a slightly more friendly tone since he and Pokey were alone.

Pokey who mostly only listened when Ram spoke just smiled and slowly nodded his head.

"Then when we get all the loot, we gon' lay and figure out a way to bust my mama out and bounce out the country. „Member how she use to take care of us when we was younger? It was just us three. That's how it's gon' be again … just us three." Ram continued with a slight smile as he reached for his car keys.

Pokey responded with only the continuous nodding of his head and the same devious smile as he got up to leave. He was nearer to the door than Ram and was there before Ram even stood. While exiting the room, Pokey was startled by a body swiftly moving down the hall then down the steps. It was Queen Nef! Pokey immediately informed Ram.

"Yo nigga, I think that bitch Queen Nef heard us talkin." Pokey explained.

"Go catch that bitch and do her like Taz. Except this time you do it and make sure the shit get done!" Ram ordered with clinched teeth and fire in his eyes.

By the time Pokey made it down stairs though, Queen Nef had already left. Herc was still standing on the porch drinking wine from the bottle.

"Yo nigga...where Queen Nef?" Pokey asked.

"Her an' some o. her bitches just pulled off in the jeep." Herc answered.

"Wha' she say before she lef.?" Pokey asked as he stared hard into Herc's eyes for a lie.

"She ain't say nothin', she just jumped in the jeep and dipped." Herc said with a shrug of his shoulders.

"Yo...I need to get wit' her. Ram don' changed up. He want Queen Nef an' those otha ' bitches ta' do shit different." Pokey said calmly.

"What about me and my niggas?" Herc asked.

"Ya'll shit's the same. Hit Nef on the celly an' tell her to meet me up at the Lot." Pokey ordered.

"F.sho." Herc responded as he pulled a cell phone from his pocket.

The Lot was an abandoned shopping center where the Mobsters handled large drug transactions. Ram, who was lurking in the shadows inside of the house, stepped out as Herc left.

"Ride around the ave an' get a few heads ta' go wit' you. E'body in that jeep wit Queen Nef gotta go. She might o. ran her mouth to 'em. Come directly back here wit' out stoppin. I'm gon need to break shit down so there won't be no questions." Ram explained as he reentered "the house."

Pokey, without saying a word, got in his Range Rover and proceeded to carry out Rams orders. Ram despised betrayal, and his punishment for betrayal was death! He was judge and jury, which meant even if the party accused of betrayal was innocent, determining such innocence was strictly up to Ram, who never investigated much. Most times if the circumstances proved one guilty, the punishment of death was imposed. His mother taught him to never question his first instinct and though sometimes this advice worked to his favor ... there were exceptions, such as Taz and Queen Nef.

Pokey, and four younger members of the gang, lay in wait as Queen Nef's jeep entered the parking lot. Pokey chose younger members, none of whom exceeded the age of thirteen, because they were merely puppets. They admired the "O.G.'s" (older gangsters) and jumped at any chance to become known. No order was questioned, especially those which came from the O.G.'s. They all sat patiently and waited for Pokey's signal. Each was armed with an automatic weapon, and their only thought was as ordered ..."Kill everyone in the jeep!"

Queen Nef, totally oblivious to the fact that she had been "marked", casually drifted to a slow halt at the entrance of the building where she was ordered to meet Pokey. She told the members who were with her to take the jeep around back, out of view and wait for her to come out. As she put the jeep in park and opened her door to get out, Pokey yelled,

"You fucked up bitch!"

This was the signal for his cronies to come out shooting. Pokey, whose main target was Queen Nef, never took his finger off of the trigger. He continued to shoot Queen Nef until she fell back into the jeep. The other members rained bullets inside the jeep. The female members kicked, screamed, and waved their arms in an attempt to block the fiery pellets consistently tearing into their bodies but it was all in vain. In seconds, the kicking and screaming ceased to where only the ping-panging of the ricocheting bullets could be heard.

The young villains, after admiring the bloody sight inside the jeep smiled at each other as their hearts raced violently from the thrill of killing. Pokey, who pulled a nine millimeter pistol from the waistline of his pants from the small of his back, randomly pumped bullets into the heads of each of the female member's … twice in Queen Nef's. Then, as if nothing had happened, he apathetically gathered his squad of assassins and deserted the scene.

After returning to "the house" where Ram explained to the young murderers how "those bitches betrayed the family," Pokey set up a small house party where the honored guests were the four young murderers who had just accompanied him on his evil mission. The mob-ettes would except the explanation that Queen Nef and the others had been killed for being "snitches" and then receive new ranks of command. And after being briefed on their role in the bank robberies, all would go on as usual.

Herc, who was intimately involved with Queen Nef and had two children with her, was not so accepting of the explanation. He had been with Pokey the night he was ordered to kill Taz yet still had not known exactly why Taz was "marked." Though he was deathly afraid of Ram and Pokey, he was not about to let Queen Nef's death go unexplained. His being blamed for not "keeping his bitch in check," was totally unacceptable. He vowed that some way, some how…somebody was going to pay for the death of his woman!

The ATL Mobsters had a membership capacity of about four hundred-fifty members in the city who were mostly all black but there were a few Puerto Ricans, Latinos, Mexicans, Asians, and Hispanics. Ram considered these all to be of the same origin … people of color. White membership was forbidden because whites were associated with "the man" or "the law." There was a white gang "Skinheads", from the outskirts of Atlanta, who once engaged in a very brief war with the Mobsters. Due to Rams dislike of whites he ordered all other business to be put to a halt so he could focus all of his attention on the Skinheads. The casualties were so great for the Skinheads, they seemed to no longer exist as a gang, and dared not tangle with the Mobsters again.

Even the police were somewhat leery of the Mobsters because under Ram's leadership, they had become not only stronger in number but also a hundred times more deadly than they had been under the leadership of his uncles. According to an unofficial investigation, it had been established that The Mobsters were responsible for more than half the murders in the city over the past few years. Though some members had been charged and sent to prison for some murders, these members were very low ranking. And due to the threat of being marked and killed by incarcerated members who were still loyal affiliates of the gang, no one was willing to tell anything. The higher ranking members were untouchable...especially Ram. Not only was he ruthless, he was smart when it came to the streets. With the aid of his mother, from federal prison, Ram had achieved a status which ranked him amongst the most infamous Mobsters in history.

The eve of the bank robberies had come and Herc was very ill tempered. He had attended the funeral of Queen Nef two days prior and was still shaken by the remnants left on his woman from the merciless attack. The casket was closed out of respect for Queen Nef's mother, an older Puerto Rican woman, who requested it that way due to the irreparable damage to her nineteen year old daughter's body. Herc was compelled to look inside the casket anyway. He had to see her just one more time. His decision was one he would live to regret. Police reports stated that over one hundred rounds had been shot into the jeep during the vicious multiple slaying. This was determined by the amount of empty shells found at the scene.

The coroner's report stated that Queen Nef had been hit with an estimated 30–40 rounds. Her long curly black hair was singed grotesquely. Her once beautiful toffee colored face had received so many bullets it was discolored and swollen to a point where it could not even be recognized as a face. Her mouth was slightly opened and through her torn lips Herc could see the ruin of broken teeth which used to make up what he considered the most beautiful smile in the world. And though Herc had witnessed death on many an occasion, seeing Queen Nef in such a condition caused him to gag so hard he had to cover his mouth to hold in the volcano of vomit which tried to make its way up his esophagus.

The removal of his hand caused the lid to slam shut, grabbing the attention of those who had not already been watching Herc brave the sight of his fallen love. How could a young woman, so gorgeous in appearance, not only have been subjected to such a life but meet such an unspeakable fate? Then as he thought, the familiar words of preachers and guidance counselors rained on him as coldly as ice droplets on a naked body. "You live by the sword, so shall you die by the sword!" For the first time in his life, fear had actually grabbed hold of his spirit, and he began to think of his own life. He was only twenty years old and, as he had done a few times before, questioned his own choice of living. A thought came to his mind which would not only hopefully change his future but would also get just revenge which was certainly called for as far as he was concerned.

As Herc sat alone in his car taking hard swigs of wine from the bottle, the tears which had come days late began to roll down his face in thin steady streams. The police precinct began to blur in his vision but he knew it was still there and he knew what he had to do. Before he said anything though, the police would have to agree to protect him, as well as moving his mother, sister, children, and Queen Nef.s mother away from the city. He would tell the police first about the bank robberies which would ensure the arrest of at least Pokey, who he knew was responsible for Queen Nef's death. Later he would tell of murders, drug transactions, and other bank robberies which would hopefully indict Ram, who ordered the hit. He would also agree to testify in exchange for his own immunity as well as his previous
demands.

Inside the precinct, Herc spoke with detectives and F.B.I. officers who had been called in to hear all he had to say.

"So Ram ordered the hit on Queen Nef?" A detective asked again.

"Yeah. I don't know why but Pokey an' some younger mobsters did it." Herc said while staring down at the table thinking of how he had reached a point of no return.

"And the two under covers?" An F.B.I. agent asked.

"Ram did it. He had me and some of my crew take those narks to this abandon buildin' in our hood. Then we tied 'em up and Ram beat 'em wit. a big chain with a big lock on the end of it. Both of 'em was already dead but Ram ordered one of the young mobsters to shoot 'em both in the head. That was the young mobsters initiation to a higher rank." Herc explained.

"How many people have you killed Herc?" Another detective

asked before having his arm grabbed by an F.B.I. agent.

Herc briefly looked at the detective, and then replied.

"Ya'll promised I wasn't goin down."

"You're not," The F.B.I. agent began, "we just need to know exactly how many hits Ram has ordered." he continued.

"Yeah well, I think that e'thing I'm telling you should be enough to knock Ram down fo' life!" Herc replied as he looked back down at the table and continued fiddling with his fingers.

"Why exactly do you want to, as you say, knock Ram down?" One detective asked.

"I told you...I'm ready ta' do the right thing." Herc answered.

"Tell us more about these bank robberies which are going to take place." The F.B.I. agent asked.

As Herc began to tell all of the details of what was to take place, agents were making phone calls to prepare for the robberies. They had planned to get as many members as possible, some of whom would hopefully do more talking. Though the deal with Herc would be upheld, F.B.I. agents, some of whom had been involved in the take down of Ram's uncles and the others, wanted as much evidence against The Mobsters as they could get. They wanted the gang broken up for good! Taking down a gang like the Mobsters would be a large and historic victory for law enforcement. Extreme and precise preparation for what would later be referred to as "The Showdown...part 2, was initiated to ensure a smoother outcome than the original "showdown"...the one involving Ram's uncles.

FBI agents, teaming with local police, manned unmarked police cars. Officers in plain clothes on foot were precisely placed in areas covering a three block radius of each bank targeted to be hit. Though Ram was not actually expected to participate in any of the robberies, detectives anticipated he may be in the vicinity of at least one of the targeted areas. Unfortunately for the detectives though, Ram was too smart for that. Obviously he was not aware of the setup which awaited his unsuspecting gang members but he usually kept his hands out of the corrupt activity which he, advised by Celeste, master minded.

The murder of the two undercover officers who had joined the ranks of the Mobsters hoping to destroy the gang from within ... that was a personal matter. Yet even in that case Ram could not take credit. Autopsy reports ruled the gunshots to the head as the cause of death in both cases. So even with Herc's testimony, Ram could only be charged with giving the order...which would exclude him from the death sentence agents had hoped the courts would impose.

Herc's absence would have aroused suspicion which could have proven detrimental to the bust, so it was agreed Herc would participate in the robbery and be arrested as well. But instead of being locked up he would immediately be taken into protective custody. His mother, sister, two children, and Queen Nef's mother had already been taken into custody and relocated to temporary housing somewhere in the mid west. Not even Herc was informed of their whereabouts until later. Queen Nef also had three brothers, all in prison, who were also not informed of where their mother was. They were all affiliated with the Mobsters and could not be trusted with the secret of their mother's location. They would in fact be made aware of the situation later but even for the sake of their mother and murdered sister, their loyalty remained. Initiated by fear ... no member could be expected to cooperate with making a case against Ram. It's strange how the psychology of gang affiliation so strongly enhances one's loyalty to the gang while at the same time destroys ones loyalty to one's own biological family.

The stage for the robberies was superbly set. F.B.I. agents had originally planned to staff all of the banks with their own people but Herc informed them that Ram had ordered his members to pay close attention to specific individuals while casing the banks. That way they could be sure there was no set up.

"Smart." One of the agents chuckled out.

"Yeah...too smart for his own good." An older detective scowled.

With the information given them, agents replaced a few employees with their own people, and also provided plain clothes officers inside and outside of each bank as support. The plan was to allow the members to enter each bank. Agents outside would seize the getaway vehicles then drive them to the designated spots where the bank robbing members would be picked up by other members and abandon the vehicle used in the robbery.

Unfortunately for them, the awaiting members would be waiting to go to jail instead of a big payday. Inside the bank there could be no mistakes. The members of the mobsters were killers and would not hesitate to shoot any or every one they could if trouble arose.

While inside the vault of one of the targeted banks, one of five agents received a message through his headset.

"Red team leader, do you read?"

"Red team leader...I read, go ahead blue team." The agent responded.

"The suspects have entered the bank and their getaway vehicle has been seized. I repeat...the suspects have entered the bank. The getaway vehicle has been seized...over!" A voiced relayed through the headset.

The agent responded

"I read, blue team." Then the agent flicked a small switch on the right side of his headset. He continued. "Red teams 1, 2, 3, 4, and 5 are you in position?"

This question set off a sequence of 5 "checks!"

"Red team 1...red team leader." A voice whispered through the headset.

"Red team leader...go on red team 1." The agent responded.

"Four suspects have taken position. Two suspects are moving toward you with the bank president...over!" The voice responded.

"Red team, move only on my signal. I repeat...move only on my signal." The agent ordered.

Robbing The National Bank of Atlanta would bring in the most profit, which is why Ram assigned Pokey to that one. It was Pokey, along with Herc, who escorted the bank president, closely and at gun point, to the vault in the back of the bank. The other four members were to get the cash from the other windows after, and only after, Pokey and Herc had finished emptying the vault into the two large duffel bags each of them carried. They would drag the bags back out to the front of the bank, after killing the bank president. The other four members would have exactly 2 minutes to get as much cash from the teller windows, and upon exiting the bank they were to holocaustically execute all bank employees as well as by-standers inside the bank.

"Leave no witnesses!" Ram previously stressed.

Knowledge of the whole plan, courtesy of Herc, made it extremely easy for agents to keep the situation from turning into a bloodbath. Upon entering the vault, the unsuspecting Pokey was quickly disarmed and laid face down inside the vault right next to Herc who tried his best to act as surprised as Pokey. The red team leader, through his headset, ordered his team members to action by simply saying

"red team, move!" ... prompting the other red team members to very efficiently disarm and take into custody the other Mobster members.

Operations at all the other banks went basically the same. It was amazing that no shots had to be fired, especially considering who was being dealt with. But also considering Herc's precise information, the outcome was to be expected. 25 members were arrested, none of whom was Ram. Also none of whom was willing to even acknowledge the fact that they knew Ram. However, even if they had, no arrest could be made. After multiple crack house raids, including "the house", Ram could not be found. He was gone! He had taken the money from previous robberies and drug transactions, and disappeared without a trace. This created a complicated situation. Ram was an extremely dangerous man. Not only did he pose a threat to Herc, who eventually through testimony would reveal his role in the arrests but also to any and everyone who got in his way. His situation was now one of desperation which made him public enemy number one on the F.B.I.'s ten most wanted list.

Chapter 15

Peter, after speaking with the Governor just days after "The showdown – part 2", realized the decision to continue the delay of the annual picnic was a wise one. Gang violence exploded in the city resulting mostly from the knowledge of Ram's disappearance. The Mobster's without Ram, Pokey, Herc, or Queen Nef were vulnerable, unorganized, and other gangs sought to exploit that fact. The lifeless bodies of mobster members were popping up all over the city. Two of Queen Nef's brothers had been beaten and stabbed to death after being found guilty by fellow gang members of having been snitches who contributed to the foiled bank robbery attempts. The third of Queen Nef's brothers lay hospitalized, in critical condition, under heavy security after he too was attacked. City police had their hands full. Then there was the search for Ram...he had to be found.

For the next 3 months, arrested Mobster members were tried and sentenced to variations of federal time ranging from 5 to15 years. Herc claimed to have no knowledge of murders any of these members may have committed. Pokey, who caught an additional stabbing charge while in a federal holding facility, was the only member indicted for any murders. He was charged with the execution style murders of Queen Nef and the other three mob-ettes, and sentenced to death...which did not seem to phase him much. He even refused to give up the younger mobsters who accompanied him on the bloody mission, and merely smiled after the judge passed sentence.

During those three months, the weather had also begun to change. It was late October which was certainly an inappropriate time to have an outdoor picnic. But who said it had to be outdoors. Though Ram was still at large, police had finally gotten the city somewhat back under control. Gang violence did still exist but after multitudes of arrests, there was a large decrease in murders. That fact, in addition to the guilt of having to delay the annual picnic, moved the Governor toward not only a change of heart but also an excellent idea. He was going to allow Peter and the "New Beginnings" organization to hold the annual picnic in the city's Civic Center downtown. Concession stands could be used as cook out areas, the stage for entertainment was already set up, and instead of sitting on the lovely green grass of Piedmont Park (which is one of the best aspects of a picnic) picnic goers would have to sit in the cushioned seats of the Civic Center. A small compromise some of the older attendants probably would not mind. The Governor relayed his proposal to Peter through a personal phone call, and after a long chummy conversation, Peter phoned Cassandra.

"Cassandra...guess what?" Peter began. Before Cassandra had an opportunity to respond, he continued. "The Governor is allowing us to hold the annual picnic at the Civic Center downtown."

"The Civic Center!?!" Cassandra exclaimed in a surprised way.

"Yes! We can use the concession stands for cookout areas, and improvise with the rest. It will be great! It will be even more memorable than any other picnic we've had." Peter explained excitedly.

"Well, it does sound a bit unusual but I've never actually heard of any rule stating picnics have to be held outside. And the concession stands do have exhaust fans so there won't be any problems with smoke." Cassandra agreed.

"That's exactly right. So let's start making calls and getting things in order. It shouldn't take much effort. I'd like to schedule the picnic to take place within the next two weeks. Thanksgiving will soon be coming up and I don't want the picnic to interfere with that!" Peter explained.

The basic arrangements for everything had already been taken care of months earlier. The biggest problem was getting the celebrities who had planned to attend to agree to rearranging their schedules for the sake of the kids. Actually the delay worked in Peter's favor because celebrities who were entertaining out of state during the original date of the picnic were now available to participate.

"God works in mysterious ways." Cassandra would continue to remind everyone she spoke with. "Only the Lord has the power to change a bad situation into something glorious and wonderful. Praise his name. Praise his name!" she'd continue while briefly raising her hands with her head tilted upward toward the sky, closed eyes, and a pleasing smile.

Peter, who was not religious, could not help but feel a bit moved by her comments and gestures. The occasion had been turned into something glorious and wonderful. He also thought of another positive aspect of the rescheduling. Tyranny and Jasmine could come for the picnic, and stay for Thanksgiving in order to get a more in depth view of Peter's life. He had not visited with them in over a month but planned to call them later that day to explain the situation.

Taz who had always dreamed of playing ball in the Civic Center was also very excited about the upcoming event. Though he would not be playing ball, he would be performing in the Civic Center which could classify as his first taste of entertaining there. Each year he and the other kids at the ranch house performed a play depicting the significantly positive effect "New Beginnings" had on their individual lives. This play was basically a motivational tool used to encourage those youth, who still lived gang affiliated or drug addicted lives, to abandon it all and take steps toward initiating change in their lives. For the most part, the intentions of "New Beginnings" proved to result in positive outcomes. But there were those individual cases where either drugs had too tight a grip on some, or gang ties gripped others. There were even some cases where either ex patriarchs would be "marked" by their ex-gang members, and severely beaten up which sometimes resulted in death. These were situations which unfortunately could not have been avoided.

During his talk with his wives, Peter began to realize just how much he missed them. His intention was to spend at least one week per month with them but because of the recent chaos in the city, Peter felt compelled to remain there just in case his assistance was needed. Though he could do nothing more to assist than to keep his kids off the streets so they would not be mistakenly targeted by the police, it was something. Now though, a large portion of the problem had been taken care of and Peter wanted to be in the company of his wives.

"Well, the picnic is scheduled to take place in two weeks. It's going to be held here at the Civic Center." Peter explained briefly.

"Sounds very interesting. I can't wait to get there. You know we've been missing you like crazy sweetheart." Jasmine said.

"Yes we have. And your suggestion that we stay and spend Thanksgiving there is a lovely one. When would you like for us to fly over?" Tyranny asked.

"Can you leave now?" Peter asked in a jokingly pleading way.

"Oh Tyranny listen to him!" Jasmine exclaimed in a compassionate way.

"I know I told you we should have made the surprise visit I suggested a few weeks back." Tyranny remarked.

"I know...I just thought he may have been busy." Jasmine responded.

"Ladies...I'm never, nor will I ever be too busy for the loves of my life." Peter cut in.

"That's so sweet." Tyranny replied.

"How about we go ahead and make arrangements for a late evening flight!?!" Jasmine suggested.

"That would be perfect! Call me and let me know what time I should meet you." Peter replied.

"We will." both Jasmine and Tyranny said almost simultaneously.

"Tyranny...I love you." Peter said softly.

"And I love you Peter." Tyranny replied in a very emotional way.

"Jasmine...I love you." Peter said in the same soft tone.

"Oh...I love you too." Jasmine replied.

"I can't wait to see you both. And don't worry about packing too much. I don't want either of you having to carry too much. We'll do some shopping while you're here...understood." Peter lovingly ordered.

"Understood." both ladies chimed with slight chuckles to follow.

"Get here soon ... okay?" Peter concluded.

For a few minutes after hanging up the phone, Peter sat stared in space contemplating how lucky he was. Not only over the fact of having two wives but two extraordinary wives. Both Tyranny and Jasmine made him extremely happy. Their expression of love toward him made it clear he made them just as happy. Though the marriage was less than 4 months old, he could easily anticipate spending the rest of his life in absolute love with his wives. Peter also discovered, contrary to popular belief, three was undoubtedly company! The very essence of life itself...the very molecule from which all creation is composed is in itself a group of three...proton, neutron, and electron. With this on his mind, it was safe for him to assume symbolically...three represented completion!

Peter smiled abruptly at the thought. He frequently amused himself with his own level of thought. As a teen he would sit for hours sometimes...just thinking and trying to figure things out. His understanding of the complexities of life is what contributed to the open-minded way with which he dealt with life. Possibility is eternal. And those who do not realize this are basically cheating themselves out of completely experiencing and enjoying life.

Jasmine and Tyranny arrived in Atlanta at nearly midnight. After picking them up, taking them to his home, and getting them settled in, Peter sat up and talked with his wives until the later hours of the morning. This was the first time the ladies had visited Peter's home, and were very impressed by what they initially witnessed. The design and structure of the house was magnificent. There were beautiful hardwood floors which shined like glass. The pine banisters and railings shined just as superbly. In the middle of the living room there spun a black iron spiraling staircase surrounding an 8-foot high indoor fountain, which featured a group of 5 brown marble sculptured people. They were holding hands with heads thrown back and eyes to the sky. There were many paintings showcased as well. Monet's, Rembrandts, and other paintings vibrantly covered the walls. Fascinating Persian rugs, antique furniture, and the many imported sculpted pieces manifested a utopia in which Tyranny and Jasmine immediately fell in love.

Both women knew Peter had excellent taste by the clothes he wore but his home shed new light on the amazing nature of this man. He was beyond incredible. It was no wonder Cassandra, who had most likely been inside Peter's home, was so much in love with him.

It was not extremely cold outside, yet Peter had been burning wood in the fire place. It set an exceptionally intimate and comfortable mood. The fire place itself, which was visually breath taking to say the least, had become a very educational topic of discussion. Peter explained how he had the entire fire place, interior and exterior, shipped from India. It was designed by a tribe of Aztecs with whom Peter had met many years prior while he vacationed there. He noticed many sculptured pieces, symbols mostly, throughout the entire reservation and desired to have some to take home as reminders of his trip. The chief explained it would be against the will of their gods for him to take any of those specific pieces but he had an idea. He described a gift he would have custom made for Peter, not only as a reminder of the trip but also as an excellent addition to the home Peter previously explained he had been decorating.

The fire place was the gift. It consisted of exterior left and right pillar shaped boundaries made with pure Ivory. There was an ancient spear in addition to an array of other Aztec symbols chiseled and painted in each. The top of the fireplace was also Ivory, centered with the shape of the head of a bald eagle, and out stretched wings which extended a few inches on both sides beyond the pillars. There were also two rounded marble steps which extended from pillar to pillar. The inner portion of the fire place was bronze with 5 brail type figures sitting cross-legged, Indian style. The figures were the chief, three other young warriors, and Peter who was placed in the center. They were all traditionally dressed, from head to toe, and appeared to be sitting around a camp fire when the logs in the fireplace were lit.

The entire piece was an absolute priceless work of art! Peter was not only surprised but greatly honored to be the recipient of such an astonishing gift. He had already had the unequaled pleasure of experiencing the outstanding intellectuality of the Indian but to be esteemed with a one of a kind hand crafted work of elegance was beyond words. Peter was eternally grateful to the Aztecs, and his opportunity to have met them.

Jasmine and Tyranny were totally absorbed in Peter's story of the origin of the fireplace, as well as his many other stories of the many other sculpted and hand crafted gifts he had received from "our people" he said with pride. Peter believed, though not admittedly religious, all people had one common origin. Whether anyone agreed or not was irrelevant because it was a fact. Both ladies agreed totally, as they did with most of Peter's philosophies. As they listened, each would slowly sip from their individual cups of cocoa when ever Peter paused to sip his. Sometimes he would sip merely to conceal the smile he could feel conjuring from the amusing appearance of his very intrigued and absolutely attentive wives. With each sip he also wondered, while continuously transferring his gaze from the beauty of Jasmine's eyes to the prototypical eyes of Tyranny, if they could see how intrigued and absolutely attentive he was toward them.

Peter was unequivocally absorbed in the magic of love, and the utopian level of emotion it manifested. Every single aspect of his wives was consumed and mentally registered whenever he as with them. The frequency of the brief separations, dictated nothing less. The hourly chime of Peter's ten foot tall grandfather clock, which he purchased at an auction in England and came with a story of its own, grabbed Peter's attention compelling him to look at his watch. It was 9 a.m.! The clock chimed 8 times prior, and he had not noticed it at all.

"Oh...ladies, I apologize. With all of my babble, I've been preventing you from resting." Peter said sympathetically.

"Rest? Sweetie we haven't seen you in over a month." Tyranny responded.

"You also must keep in mind that this is our very first trip to visit you. And it is very apparent, by the looks of this gorgeous house," Jasmine began while looking around, "we still have a lot to learn about our fabulous husband." she continued.

"Exactly. We can rest later." Tyranny concluded.

"What about your pregnancies?" Peter asked in a concerned way.

"Honey," Jasmine began as she walked over to where Peter was sitting, put both her hands gently on both of his cheeks, then lightly kissed him on the lips. "We're fine." she continued.

"We have an excellent doctor...remember?" Tyranny began, as she walked over and hugged Peter around his neck from behind while at the same time lightly nibbling on his ear.

"There is one thing we could both use." Tyranny continued as she began to rub Peter's broad chest.

"Oh...you mean what we discussed on the plane." Jasmine said as she straddled Peter's lap.

"Is that right." Peter replied as he began to gently caress the contours of Jasmine's body.

"Yes...that's right. You've been neglected for over a month, and we'd like to make up for it." Tyranny answered as she began opening the buttons of Peter's shirt to reveal his mind blowing bulk!

"Well if you'll both wait here a brief moment, I.ve got to get something for the occasion." Peter said as he helped Jasmine off his lap and headed up the spiral staircase.

"Hurry back." Tyranny yelled up after him.

A few minutes later, Peter returned with a large comforter and a chilled bottle of sparkling white grape juice.

"We won't be needing this right now." Jasmine remarked as she took the bottle from Peter's hand. Tyranny in turn took the comforter and spread it out in front of the fireplace, and in seconds, all three were enjoying an abundance of foreplay which eventually led to hours of love making which lasted into the middle of the afternoon.

"Are you satisfied sweetheart." Jasmine said softly in between gentle kisses of Peter's lips.

"I sure hope so!" Tyranny, who was cuddled next to Peter opposite Jasmine, replied setting off short laughter between the three.

"Baby...you are one hell of a man." Jasmine pointed out.

"Yes, you are! I have just enough energy left to get showered and dressed. You two will probably have to carry me around for the whole day." Tyranny said jokingly.

"Well...don't sell yourselves short. I'm more than satisfied even when we're just talking." Peter responded.

After getting dressed, Peter decided the first stop would be somewhere to have a late lunch. He tried to think of a healthy restaurant but the ladies explained how they had been eating "rabbit food" for months, and wanted real food. Madeline gave them permission to cheat a little, so they decided on fast food! Later they headed to one of Peter's downtown centers to meet some of the kids. On the way they passed by the Civic Center where the annual picnic would be held, while also passing the professional football stadium where Peter promised to take them during a game before they went back to L.A.. Neither women knew a thing about football but admittedly enjoyed seeing the butts of the players. Peter chuckled, while pulling out his cell phone. There was a brief pause then in a matter of seconds, he booked box seats right at the 50 yard line. He even promised, with visual amusement, to have binoculars in order to increase the view. The ladies were thrilled, showing it by hugging and kissing Peter, which caught the attention of the driver. After seeing how he was watching them more than the road, Peter nonchalantly raised the automatic non-transparent glass petition. Both ladies quickly realizing the situation apologized. Peter in turn encouragingly explained that there was no need for apologies from them. Actually it was he who owed them apologies for asking them to keep their marriage concealed.

"Eventually though," Peter began. "all will be out in the open. And the sooner the better," he continued.

Peter purposely avoided going to the ranch house, not only because it was the ladies first day but because he was not ready for them to meet Cassandra. She meant a lot to him, and though he was not intimately interested in her, he felt guilty due to his knowledge of how she felt about him. He did call her though and explained the state of affairs! Two friends from L.A. would be visiting the following day and he wanted to bring them by the house. Cassandra was pleased to have been informed in advance, considering the fact that she and the kids would have time to prepare a presentable house and a nice southern style meal. The meal was Peter's idea. Jasmine and Tyranny loved southern style "soul food". Back in L.A., Isabella made sure the ladies received a sufficient amount of it. Both women themselves were also excellent cooks, and could 'burn" (a word used by some southerners which basically meant cook very well) just as well as any southern woman could. But to eat a southern style meal, while actually in the south, was an experience.

The south has a complexity composed of many aspects...some of which were disliked by non southerners but tolerated due to the understanding of their origins. The other aspects such as the "old fashioned" values which unified families seemed almost magical...especially at meal times. Meals prepared with that certain southern something seemed to be an antidote for anything. Family disagreements, broken friendships, marital problems...it did not matter. Southern "fixins" could fix it.

Tyranny and Jasmine looked forward to visiting the ranch house because it was another piece of their husband's life which they were eager to learn. They also could not wait to meet Cassandra. Peter explained how she was a wonderful woman...very kind hearted and compassionate but she was extremely fond of him and tended to display slight jealousy whenever other women seemed closer to him than she was. Neither Jasmine nor Tyranny was thrilled over the fact that they would have to humbly accept any "attitude" deriving from feelings of possessiveness over a man who they themselves already had. In any other circumstance they would kindly tell her off and leave it at that but this predicament was delicate for reasons other than Cassandra herself.

There were also the kids to think about, as well as Peter's reputation. Not that either expected his reputation to be ruined by his marriage. However, both women knew how cruel the "socially rebellious" were discriminated against. They endured many years of conditioning which contributed to the care free attitude both women had in reference to the opinions of others about their marriage. Cassandra could display her jealousy with no retaliation from either of Peter's friends from L.A.. If things got out of hand though, he promised to handle it.

The next day, as Peter rolled up over the hill, the ranch house grew into view. Both Tyranny and Jasmine were surprised at how similar in appearance it was to the ranch houses across the border in Tijuana, Mexico. With all of his stories of travel, the ladies almost expected Peter to explain how he got the design for the ranch house from there.

"Actually," Peter began, "the ranch house was already there when I purchased the land. The only work we had to do was cut down all of the trees that were here, till the ground, add the recreation area, and do other minor renovations. The house itself was a mess at first but a nail here and a nail there, and...walla!" Peter continued with a smile.

The previous afternoon, while Peter and his wives were leaving his home, a small group of neighborhood children were playing outside and greeted them. The ladies had the pleasure of experiencing Peter's effect on children. Then at the center with the older kids, the ladies experienced the effect once again. So, as they drove up into the premises of the ranch house, the reaction of the kids was no surprise. Also as expected by Peter, at the sight of the two gorgeous guests Peter brought with him, the guys turned suddenly into distinguished gentlemen. Taz even tried to make his voice deeper when he said

"How are you Peter? It's great to see you. And who may I ask are these lovely young ladies?"

The question got an immediate eyebrow raising smile from both Jasmine and Tyranny but a hard slap on the arm from Lena who followed it with a very mean scowl.

"All right Barry White, cool your engines." Cassandra, who also surprised by Peter's guests, began as she made her way passed the kids to introduce herself to the ladies."Hello...my name is Cassandra. I'm the supervising counselor here at New Beginnings." She continued in a proper and articulately professional voice while extending her hand first to Tyranny then to Jasmine.

"Cassandra... Hi I'm Tyranny and this is my wi...uh, companion Jasmine." Tyranny responded, triggering a racing of heart beats with her slight slip of tongue.

"Yes, we're acquaintances of Peter's from L.A.." Jasmine followed.

"Peter...no wonder you've been going away to L.A. so often. Two beautiful women? And all this time we've been worrying that you were lonely on your trips." Cassandra replied in a politely phony way through a very obvious forced smile which had more clinch than curve.

"Cassandra, Jasmine and Tyranny helped me get things together for the ranch house in L.A.." Peter explained.

"Oh...so these are business associates?" Cassandra asked sarcastically.

"Yes we are." Tyranny responded with a bland smile which clearly indicated her displeasure with Cassandra's attitude.

Jasmine, in an attempt to smooth things over blurted out,

"We couldn't wait to meet you and the kids...we've heard so much about you."

"Is that right? Funny...Peter never mentioned a thing about either of you." Cassandra replied cutting her eyes at Peter as she turned to walk away.

Tyranny slightly opened her mouth in an obvious attempt to fire back at Cassandra but before she had a chance to speak, Cassandra ordered the kids inside to finish preparing dinner. After she and the kids entered the house Peter began to speak.

"Ladies...I sincerely apologize. I didn't know it was going to be this bad. We can nix this whole idea if you'd like."

"Oh nooo!" Tyranny sang. "We came here to get acquainted and that's what we're going to do." She continued.

"I agree with Tyranny. That woman has got it bad for you sweetheart but you're our husband! The only way we're going to move closer toward revealing this fact is by confronting her and her attitude!" Jasmine said sternly.

"I can respect that but I don't want to make a scene...especially not in front of the kids." Peter responded.

Both women were briefly silent. Then with deep breaths, both exhaled.

"No scene." Jasmine said calmly, as she looked at Tyranny for an agreeable response.

"Okay!" Tyranny began with a slight pout."But can I at least pull her off to the side and give her a piece of my mind if she continues her rude behavior?" she continued.

"As long as you do it as tactfully as I know you can." Peter began. "I plan to talk to her myself when we go inside so your „piece of mind giving. may not be necessary." he continued.

The aroma of fried chicken had already made its way outside but as Peter, Tyranny, and Jasmine entered the house the additional smells of broccoli and scalloped potatoes smothered in melted cheddar & Swiss cheese aroused the forgotten hunger in all of their bellies. It was very "homey" inside, not only due to the mouth watering smells in the air but also the neatness. At first glance it would be impossible to know eight teenagers resided there.

Cassandra's attitude had also changed. Contemplating the conversation with Jasmine and Tyranny, she was forced to realize how wrong she was for acting so rudely toward the ladies. She was a Christian woman whose religious and spiritual upbringing dictated her walk be much more dignified and humble than her earlier display of character suggested. She had planned to hopefully amend her earlier actions by first apologizing to both ladies, then treating them in the respectful way which guests should be treated. Regardless of the fact Peter never mentioned the gender of his L.A. associates.

Tyranny and Jasmine very skeptically took seats on the sofa which appeared as if it had never been sat on before. Peter, disturbed greatly by Cassandra's behavior, went directly into the kitchen where Cassandra and the kids were. All of the kids were unusually quiet, and only looked silently at each other as Peter entered. They were not so young as to not know what was going on in regards to Cassandra's jealousy. Cassandra, noticing the blatant look of displeasure on Peter's face, spoke up immediately in hopes of halting what she anticipated would be a verbally wrathful chastising. He had never actually done so in her case but she witnessed it once before when Peter unleashed his wrath on a counselor who had vulgarly insulted one of his kids at the center. No one had ever seen Peter so furious and actually feared seeing a violent side of him. But Peter was more man than that, and had enough discipline to not only refrain from such unnecessary brutality but also to realize his actions, at all times,

were to parallel his words. Before Peter could say anything, Cassandra spoke.

"Peter...can you please ask Jasmine and Tyranny to come in here? I have something I'd like to say to them." She said in as humble and sweet a voice as possible.

Peter looked carefully at Cassandra before being prompted into action by the additional "please," she softly leaked out, did as she asked. Without a word, as Tyranny and Jasmine entered the kitchen, Cassandra went and hugged each of them. Then, while gently taking hold of each of their hands, she walked them both to the table and seated them in chairs which would be on both sides of the chair she would be sitting in. The children only smiled at this action because this was the Cassandra they all knew and loved. And after seating the ladies, she took a standing position on the opposite side of the table where all attention was on her.

"Ladies," Cassandra began, giving a nod of acknowledgement to each. "I would like to apologize for my behavior outside, and I sincerely beg both your forgiveness. There is no excuse for the way I acted but hopefully I haven't done irreconcilable damage. I am a devout Christian woman who knows better but I am also a human being who sometimes falls short of what is expected of me. My Lord though, he knows my heart, and he hesitates not when I have fallen and need his all mighty hand to help me up. We've prepared what I pray turns out to be a lovely meal for you, and we'd like to offer it in peace." she continued while smiling a gentle smile.

"I think I speak for the both of us when I say you are certainly forgiven." Jasmine responded.

"That's right, we understand totally. We all sometimes act other than ourselves because as you pointed out...we are human. But what makes us better is our willingness to admit our wrong doings." Tyranny added.

"Amen. Are you ladies Christians?" Cassandra asked as both ladies got up and rounded the table to give Cassandra a forgiving hug.

"Yes." Tyranny answered after shooting a quick glance at Jasmine, "We were both raised as Christians." she continued. This was actually not a lie. Though Tyranny's religious background was more extreme and regular, Jasmine's parents merely tried to instill Christian values in her as a child by occasionally sending her to church with relatives. The one thing both women intentionally failed to mention is that neither, as adults, lived nor desired to live Christian lives. Both regarded religion as a psychologically oppressive institution which allowed very little room for individual thinking. Many would argue how religion, on the contrary, had allowed for too much individual thinking which has been the contributing force toward the very apparent absence of the aspect of morality. Regardless of any argument, the ladies had proven time and time again how they did not base their lives on what was socially accepted, rejected, or neglected. They lived their lives according to what made them happy. They did their best to avoid intentionally affecting anyone in a negative way, and in turn expected reciprocating treatment! Treat others as you yourself expect to be treated!

Dinner, according to Jasmine and Tyranny was delicious. The extensive conversation afterward was delightful, and gave the ladies an opportunity to get very acquainted with the kids and Cassandra. It was as if they had all known each other for years. Tyranny and Jasmine were people's people who dealt with many different personalities daily in each of their individual careers. Each mingled easily due to their open minded willingness to relate. Prejudice, from any standpoint, was something they tried very hard to exclude from their characters considering each had firsthand knowledge of the manifested pain. The familiarity with that pain contributed to the ladies' unwillingness to impose it on anyone else.

The kids were completely absorbed by the ladies, and even Cassandra had fallen victim to their magnetic spell. She was very impressed by the inspirationally positive way Tyranny spoke to the kids. Cassandra noted how comfortably Tyranny mingled with the kids, and was surprised due to her sophistication and beauty, of how street wise she was. There was little about the streets unknown to Tyranny. She had clients from all walks of life, who kept her in the loop in regards to just about everything from drug dealing in back alleys to investments on Wall Street. Not to mention, Tyranny had a past. She was very familiar with gangs due to the fact that while in her teens, she briefly dated a female gang member.

Cassandra was also very impressed by Jasmine's extreme intellect and her career. All of the girls at the home listened attentively as Jasmine preached on about how they should not impose limitations on themselves just because they were "young ladies." The sparkling glare in each of the "young ladies" eyes was an indication of how each was surely feeling Jasmine's vibe. Jasmine also treated the guys, who she felt were being neglected in the conversation, with very innocent and sophisticated flirtatious glances coupled with encouraging compliments. She knew how easily she could influence men...regardless of age, and she understood clearly the validity and effect her compliments were to men. So in this case, she used this tactic as a means to motivate them to live more positive lives.

It had begun to get very late, and Peter explained how it was time for the kids to get themselves prepared for bed. He also pointed out how Jasmine and Tyranny had gotten very little rest in the past two days, and they would need to get some for the upcoming events. Neither woman complained about Peter's explanation because they were in fact a bit rest needy. So after plenty of hugs and "see you tomorrows," the three were on their way back to Peter's place where they almost immediately went to bed. Peter had provided a separate room for his wives but they opted to sleep in his large bed with him. He was their husband, and father of their expected children. Being away from him for approximately three weeks of every month was enough. They felt as though sleeping in separate rooms, or even beds for that matter, while they were all together was somewhat extreme. Peter deserved as much affection as they had given each other. Actually, both ladies put forth extra effort to make the experience that much more pleasurable for their man.

For the next couple of days, Peter made sure Tyranny and Jasmine had very frequent contact with Cassandra and the kids at the ranch house, staff members and kids from the other centers, as well as other residents around Atlanta who were close affiliates of Peter's. He wanted to familiarize all of these people with Jasmine and Tyranny so the characters of both women could be known. By knowing the women more personally, Peter figured, those who knew him would be more accepting of his marriage. Both women realized this as well, which is why each of them displayed themselves openly. Well...almost openly. But eventually, even the concealed aspect would be revealed.

The day of the annual picnic had come, and just as everyone Had anticipated it was spectacular. There were musical performances by world renowned R&B artists, lectures by religious leaders and other guest speakers who were active participants in the fight to save the city's youth, poetry recitals, a talent show, two plays, and lots of eating! Jasmine and Tyranny also spoke individually, giving inspirational words of encouragement. The amazing thing about it is that neither had previously prepared any speeches, nor did they discuss it with each other. They were both a hit! Everyone absolutely adored them. They shook hands and traded phone numbers with what seemed to be hundreds of women. And though they enjoyed every minute of the attention, which they were basically used to receiving, during a brief intermission when they were off by themselves they spoke of the irony behind how kindly they were treated. How friendly will these same people be when they find out not only about the marriage but also the fact that Tyranny and Jasmine were married to each other before they became acquainted with Peter. It was not actually a sad thought because neither woman felt a desire to affiliate themselves with close minded people. What was sad was the fact that in this society, religious beliefs, color, or sexual preference out weighed character, intelligence, or integrity. It was all something both women had grown to tolerate but it was still strange how the magnificent beauty of diversity was at the same time the very factor which revealed the grotesque ugliness of mankind.

As the picnic slowly spiraled to a close, it was difficult not to smile. All of the joy and laughter created an atmosphere with an energetic potency that was powerful enough to tickle the spirit.

"This is what is it's all about". Peter contemplated to himself as he admired the whole scene. He was basically feeding off of the love and unified effort of such an abundance of people.

Even the whites, who attended, hugged and kissed blacks on their cheeks as if they unaware of the falsely standardized code of separation imposed by society. Peter recognized ex-gang members who shook hands and spoke compassionately with ex rival gang members. Recovering adolescent drug addicts, some of whom had even attempted suicide, smiled and appeared happy to be alive. Peter also noticed how Cassandra, Jasmine, and Tyranny congregated closely together, enjoying each others company like sisters who had not seen each other in years. It was all so lovely. Peter would record the day, and place it on permanent file in the back of his mind as one of the most significant occasions in his life.

The scene days later at the large Thanksgiving meal held at the downtown center, a superb encore to the annual picnic, would also be recorded in Peter's memory. It was such times which made his efforts worthwhile. Earlier that day while serving the homeless, which is how Thanksgiving Day always started at the center, Peter took pictures of an apron and chef hat wearing Taz. Taz was working the serving line for the second year in a row...and did it with pride because it made him feel as though he was making a difference. He blushed whenever some of the homeless women would compliment him on his handsome appearance and his kind heart. He was more moved by the "kind heart" compliment because Peter, who Taz admired more than any other person in the world, was also known for his.

For the next few months, Tyranny and Jasmine visited Atlanta almost as frequently as Peter visited L.A., and both had become more or less a part of the community. Both had taken maternity leave from their jobs, though they did make themselves easily accessible in case of any emergency. Being owner of her own chain of salons, Tyranny was a little more actively involved in her career during her leave than Jasmine was but most of her work consisted of paperwork. By this time, which was approximately seven months into both pregnancies, both ladies were showing. Some people had noticed earlier but kept their prying limited to behind the back questioning. Many were curious to know about husbands! The rings were there but no one had neither met nor heard of either woman's husband. Well...at least they thought they had not. Maybe, considering the sophistication of both women, their husbands were big time millionaires who stayed so busy that the women supported each other!

"You know how those rich people are." Some of the older women would gossip.

As Peter began to slowly catch wind of all the talk, he realized his months of concealing must now come to a close. It was time to be honest and reveal his marriage. He decided he would first reveal it to Cassandra and the kids at the ranch house. Regardless of what would be said, he had to let them know not only for the purpose of honesty but also respecting the sanctity of his marriage. From the time Peter stepped into the house with Jasmine and Tyranny were well aware of his decision to reveal the marriage and agreed totally. Cassandra could tell by Peter's body language something was going on. She immediately spoke up.

"What is it Peter?" Cassandra began softly, "You look very disturbed about something. Are you ill?" she continued.

"No...I'm not ill but I am a bit disturbed. Not by anything anyone else has done but because of what I've been doing. I've not been totally honest with you or anyone else in this city for that matter but I'm here to come clean." Peter began to explain causing Cassandra to look at both Tyranny and Jasmine in a very concerned and worried way."Will you please get the kids down here so I may talk to you all?" he continued as he moved to remove the coats of his wives, while simultaneously seating them both on the sofa.

Cassandra, at the same time, quickly acted on Peter's request. When all of the kids were seated, Peter began to speak.

"Cassandra, please...sit." He began, at which time Cassandra quietly yet skeptically sat in a lounge chair. "For a while now, I've been deceiving you all. My motive for such behavior was due to my extreme love for you all. You all love me too...right?" He asked briefly, which received collective "of course" responses from everyone. "Well...I feared losing that love which is why I opted to keep this secret. I never meant to hurt any of you, nor do I want what I have to say to change anything between any of us. I have given and will continue to give my all to you all. But just as you all have your own personal lives, I to have mine. So, with no further delay..." Peter continued to explain as he pulled his two wedding rings from his coat pocket and put them on his finger, "I'd like to inform you all that I'm married!" he concluded.

Silence filled the room as all of the kids looked back and forth between each other. Jasmine and Tyranny continued to sit quietly while allowing everything to play out. They knew Peter was not yet finished. Cassandra, who was caught some where between hurt and surprise, sat frozen while staring quietly at Peter. All of the kids knew exactly why Cassandra was so quiet, and remained quiet themselves.

"That's not all," Peter began calmly once again, "If you'll notice, I have two rings. That's because I do in fact have two wives!" Peter continued, causing the mouths of all the kids to practically drop open. Then without hesitation, all eyes were on Tyranny and Jasmine.

"You two?" Cassandra slightly choked out as she pointed left to right a motioning finger at the ladies.

"Yes Cassandra." Jasmine answered while Tyranny only nodded her head.

"Lord Jesus!" Cassandra exclaimed as tears began to pour uncontrollably from her eyes. "Peter how could you! Why would you! I guess you are the father of those babies inside of their bellies?" Cassandra continued angrily.

"Yes I am." Peter answered.

"I hope you realize what you've done. Sowing your wild oats! Have you lost your mind or does it now reside in your pants?" Cassandra remarked in a somewhat composed rage.

"Wait just a minute Cassandra! Not only are you blowing this out of proportion, your last comment was way out of line." Tyranny cut in defensively.

"First of all hussy, I'm not speaking to you I'm speaking to Peter! So if you don't mind...shut up!" Cassandra replied in a more heated up manner.

"Uh, Cassandra," Jasmine began as she gently grabbed the slowly charging Tyranny's hand and pulled her back down on the couch, "there is no need for name calling...understand? This marriage...it exists whether you accept it or not. The purpose of Peter telling you was not for any purposes of approval! You do not have a right to throw this childish tantrum, nor do you have the right to judge us!" Jasmine pointed out in a chastising way.

"Don't you dare tell me what I have a right to do! I have known this man for many years, and I know that there is more here than meets the eye! Obviously you two sex crazed witches have recognized the goodness of this man and came up with a way to trap him into marriage." Cassandra replied sternly.

"You've been warned once about the name calling Cassandra." Tyranny cut in.

"Ladies! Stop it!" Peter yelled with a thunderous roar that not only silenced everyone but instilled a terror which caused everyone's heart to race. "This is not what I came here for! Kids...you all go on up stairs. I'll be up there in a minute." Peter continued as he watched the kids hurriedly run up the stairs. "I am surprised at the three of you! How could three such classy ladies be carrying on in such a way? Well? You all had so much to say a minute ago! Talk now!" Peter continued angrily.

"I'm finished talking to them! You stand there and have the nerve to say you're surprised! How dare you Peter! Damn you! You know how much I love you and you go and pull a stunt like this? Damn you!" Cassandra yelled between sobs as she walked hurriedly to her room.

"Cassandra … you come back here so we can talk." Peter ordered in a less threatening and almost broken up tone.

"I am not one of your whores to be ordered around." Cassandra replied calmly as she stopped, whipped around and shot an evil glance at Peter. "And one more thing...you remember your responsibility to those kids up there!" she continued before she went in her room and slammed the door shut behind her.

Peter was frozen. He had no idea Cassandra would have reacted in such a way. He expected her to be a bit more composed but he had to admit, even to himself, her reaction made it clear how the news of his marriage would catch people off guard. The ball was rolling now though, and regardless of how people would react, the existence of his marriage would be made known.

Peter continued to stand quietly for a moment as he contemplated what he would say to the kids. Jasmine and Tyranny stared at him sympathetically. They could feel his pain. They knew almost exactly what he was going through but neither said a word. This painful "initiation" went with the territory, and unfortunately, he would have to endure it. Peter would also have to accept the fact that this was only the very beginning of what he would experience throughout his socially labeled 'immoral marriage.' It was a subject discussed very thoroughly by the three, and it was something Peter said he could deal with. Now it was time to prove it. Actually though, his most painful opposition would be Cassandra and his biggest challenge his kids. This is why he chose to tell them first. Dealing with anyone else would be no problem. First he had to deal with his kids, and then, after he allowed her to cool off a bit, Peter would once again speak privately with Cassandra.

While Peter was upstairs with the kids, Tyranny and Jasmine spoke diligently about how they would comfort Peter. He would need all of the support they could possibly give. Their own anger was basically nothing because it was all a rerun of what they had gone through many times before. They certainly did not enjoy being called names but mere words were about as damaging to them as a cold winter breeze would be to a concrete wall! Peter's feelings were their primary focus at the present time, and both women agreed they would help their husband get through this.

"Look Pete..." Taz began as he waited for Peter to finish speaking. "we were talking before you came up here, and we all agree that your personal life is your own personal business. The only thing we care about is you continuing to be here for us." he continued, as the other kids nodded their heads in agreement.

"That's right you've always taught us to live our own lives according to our own standards. And whether anyone else agrees is irrelevant, as long as we can look at ourselves in a mirror and honestly be satisfied with ourselves." Lena added.

"I did say that didn't I? Peter replied with a smile.

"Ms. Cassandra will eventually get over it. She just needs some time." Rochelle chimed in.

"You think so?" Peter asked solemnly.

"I know so! You know how us women are." Rochelle answered, setting off a room full of slight laughter.

"I'm glad you kids are okay with this. You all know how much you all mean to me, and I'd never want to do anything to change things between us. For the rest of my life, I will remain dedicated to all of you because I love you. No marriage or anything else will change that...understand?" Peter explained.

"Yes." All of the kids chimed.

"Good. Now, I need to speak with Cassandra again. I'd like to ask you all to let her know that. I'd appreciate it if she would give me a call within the next few days." Peter explained. "And if there's nothing else any of you need to talk about I'm going to head on home." he continued.

Tyranny and Jasmine immediately stood up as Peter reentered the living room. Neither of them said a word, they just smiled comforting smiles at Peter. When he smiled back, both women realized things upstairs had not gone so bad, and Jasmine spoke up.

"Everything go okay sweetheart?" She asked in a very soft and easy way.

"As a matter of fact, all went better than I had anticipated. I was also counseled by receiving past words of my own counseling." Peter answered.

"Well...what are we going to do about her?" Tyranny asked as she slightly tossed her head in a pointing gesture toward Cassandra's room.

"Actually I'm going to do nothing. I'm going to give her some time to think then I'll speak with her again...alone! I think it would also be wise if you three were not in each other's company for awhile. At least until Cassandra has an opportunity to digest the news." Peter explained.

"And what if she never does?" Jasmine asked.

"Then that's on her. I anticipate, regardless of any ill feelings she may hold onto, eventually her maturity and spirituality will help her to refrain from making a scene whenever she is in both your company...which actually won't be very often anyway." Peter explained.

"So … what now?" Tyranny asked.

Peter stepped closer to both ladies with each of his hands extended toward each of them. As each took hold, he gently pulled them closer to him.

"What we will do now," he began as he bent slightly to lightly kiss Tyranny on her lips, "is go home," he continued as he repeated the same action with Jasmine, "and relax. You two have had a long day, and you need some rest." he concluded.
Both women could do nothing more than smile with pleasure

and embrace Peter. He was a very strong and considerate man. Even in a time of despair, he never forgot the fact that his pregnant wives needed him. He tried catering to all of their needs, constantly reminding them of how beautifully they wore pregnancy, and made frequent and very emotional love to each of them to prove his words were sincere.

For the following two months, Peter performed his duties at the centers and the home, and also finally got the L.A. home staffed and opened. The L.A. home required much of his time, which meant with his obligation to his marriage he spent most of the two months in L.A.. Cassandra interpreted this as neglect to the kids at the Atlanta home and developed even more animosity toward Tyranny and Jasmine, even though the kids understood. Cassandra blamed the ladies, more than Peter, for the whole situation. Peter called very regularly, yet Cassandra refused to discuss the matter. She kept any conversation with Peter limited to the operation of the home, while maintaining a cold tone which blatantly indicated she was still angry. Peter never pushed, he only hoped the whole scenario would soon play itself out so the two of them could resume the type of relationship they had before he revealed his marriage to her. He considered Cassandra to be a very dear friend and he did not want to lose that.

As far as the many other associates Peter had throughout Atlanta, many of them accepted Peter's news gracefully. They regarded the marriage as his own personal business, and never noticed any change in his character. Of those who did not accept it, voicing their disapproval was done discreetly. The morality of the marriage was questioned but this was not really the issue. Peter was an extremely eligible bachelor before his marriage to Jasmine and Tyranny but now he was taken and many women were merely jealous! Even if he had only one wife...some people would have still spoken negatively about it.

On a very warm mid April evening, Tyranny and Jasmine lay comfortably together on a fluffy goose down comforter laid out on the living room floor in front of their big screen television. The ladies were enjoying a romantic movie Peter had earlier rented for them, while he prepared dinner. For days prior, both ladies had been experiencing light kicks, and other pains, which were explained by Madeline as having been signs of a nearing delivery. So with this in mind, Peter made sure bags were packed...just in case.

As the women lay quietly, Tyranny was the first to experience the excruciating stomach pains which caused her to literally double over. She had prepared herself mentally for this day but unfortunately reality struck and it was a bit more than she could bear. She began to cry silently as she held her stomach, while clamping her legs tightly together when she felt the extreme moisture between her legs. Her water had broken! Even with the indescribable pain she managed to strain out the words,

"It's time!" followed by more soft crying.

Jasmine, who had been holding Tyranny the whole time, was emotionally stricken by Tyranny's small battle, and began to cry to herself as tears ran uncontrollably down her pregnancy swollen face.

"Peter! Sweetheart! Tyranny's going into labor! We have to get her to the hospital!" Jasmine was yelling as Peter began to automatically take action. "Peter! Peter!" Jasmine continued as Peter quietly walked in the living room and gently took hold of Jasmine.

"Sweetheart, calm down okay?" He said calmly as he helped Jasmine to her feet while briefly looking her directly in the eyes until she nodded acceptingly. Peter then knelt down beside Tyranny.

"Sweetheart," He began calmly, "everything is going to be fine okay?" he continued as he gently ran his hand through Tyranny's hair looking for a response.

Tyranny, as she looked up at Peter with her tear soaked face, nodded continuously through the hic-up type convulsions which normally follow a hard cry. She tried hard to halt her crying and concentrated hard on Peter's gentle eyes as he helped her stand up.

"Okay now," Peter began as he got Tyranny, who seemed to have forgotten about her pain, on her feet. "We learned about all of this in class, remember?" he continued, still in a soft voice as he kept supportive eye contact with Tyranny.

"Yes...I remember." Tyranny replied softly.

"Okay, I'm going to lift you in my arms and take you down to the car." Peter said reassuringly.

"Alright." Tyranny replied as she prepared herself to be picked up

Peter, in turn, bent down and lifted Tyranny in his arms as if she were weightless.

"Hold on tightly sweetheart." Peter instructed with a reassuring smile.

Tyranny smiled back but said nothing. She merely did as Peter asked and buried her head in his strong chest. As he walked with her out the door, Tyranny called,

"Jasmine!"

"I'm right here honey." Jasmine answered from behind Peter, while quickly maneuvering herself around him into Tyranny's view.

"I'm okay...okay?" Tyranny said with a slight smile while wiping the tears from her own face.

"Okay sweetie." Jasmine responded.

Down the elevator and into the awaiting limo the three went. Tyranny, who refused to let go of Peter, sat across his lap in the wide back seat, while he rocked her, rubbed her and spoke soft gentle words of encouragement in her ear. Jasmine made the call to Madeline who immediately called the hospital, so when the three arrived, a medical team was already there. They quickly laid Tyranny on a gurney and hurriedly took her to a delivery room. A nervous Peter was sweating profusely, expected to sit with Jasmine in the waiting room and relax for a while. To his surprise though, when he turned to say something to Jasmine, she was doubled over grabbing her stomach, looking up toward Peter with a straining look on her face as if she was trying to say something.

"Sweetheart!" Peter exclaimed as he moved to her aid, "You too?" he continued as he squatted to look in her eyes.

"Yes," Jasmine cried, "my water just broke." she continued.

A nurse, who was behind the waiting room desk, had already begun to push a wheelchair over to retrieve Jasmine. Before Peter could call for anyone the nurse was there.

"Here sir, help her in this chair." the nurse began calmly. "I'll wheel her back to a delivery room and call a doctor in." she continued.

"Peter, I want to be in the same room with Tyranny." Jasmine cried.

"Nurse, can that be arranged? Please? I'd like for my wives to be together during delivery." Peter explained.

"Uh," the nurse replied after giving Peter a strange and confused look, "I imagine we can do that...under the circumstances." the nurse continued.

While standing in the delivery room, Peter would remember later the soft agonizing moans of which he alternately directed his attention. Then...after what seemed to be an eternity, a baby crying ... then another baby crying ... signified the successful entrance of Peter's, Jasmine's, and Tyranny's first children into the world. Two adorable baby girls had now made Peter a father. And if things were not strange enough, a doctor's statement would later shock all three.

"Uh...Mr. Phontane, we are aware of your marriage. We are also aware of the fact that you are obviously the father of both children. I'm sure you understand how surprised the knowledge of these facts would make the average person but sir ... that's nothing compared to what we've discovered about your two daughters." A doctor explained.

"Please don't tell me there's something wrong." Peter replied.

"No...I wouldn't say wrong, just strange," The doctor responded.

"Well what is it?" Peter asked.

"Sir...your daughters are, um...they're identical twins!" The doctor replied.